A CHOF OF CHAOS

A HORROR ANTHOLOGY

BY CHRISTOPHER JOYCE

CAPTAIN CUPCAKE
THE BONE FAIRY
CHILDREN OF THE MOUNTAIN
FILM NOIRE
IN THE UNDERGROWTH
THE RECURRING NIGHTMARE
THE MIDNIGHT MAN
THE CHAIR
THE FARMER'S WIFE
PETER'S RABBITS
SLEEPING DOGS
ROM
OF CHRISTMAS PAST
HALL OF MIRRORS
SUPER MAX
THE NEW GUY
LYDIA
UNEXPECTED ITEM
THE DOLLMAKER

To Paul,

I hope you enjoy a good scare!

Chris J.

CAPTAIN CUPCAKE

Zach Robley thought the results were starting to show. Nobody else did; his colleagues in the office certainly didn't. Earlier that day he had overheard - again - the loud-mouthed bitch in the corner snicker as he attempted to heave his bulk out of his chair and away from his desk.

"I'm gonna go grab a coffee if anybody wants anything bringing back?" he had announced. Nobody did.

"No thanks…." they said as one, with a stray "*Wobbly Robley*" thrown in for good measure when they thought he was out of earshot, giggling in twos and threes. No different to any other day really, and he was used to it by now.

Still, he had decided to try and do something about it and had recently bought himself a pair of running trainers and some new shorts. He was now wearing these as he sweated and panted his way down Birch Grove under the cover of darkness, illuminated at regular intervals only by the harsh yellow streetlights above.

Around fifteen minutes after he had set off from the doorstep of the small but well-kept house in which he lived alone, he was back and panting with his hands on his knees and eyes squeezed shut.

I'll show 'em, he thought to himself.

I'll fucking show 'em all.

Having dragged himself out of bed early, Zach spent ten minutes lifting his blue plastic dumbbells, though he could not manage much weight at the moment. He may have been a large guy, but he lacked in actual strength. Though he ached terribly from the after-effects of the previous night's run coupled with his morning workout, he tried a few push-ups on his gym mat and found that he could now manage seven, which was an improvement on last week, at least.

He showered once he had managed to catch his breath, before helping himself to a tall glass of orange juice and a banana from his well-stocked pantry for breakfast. From said pantry, Zach packed himself a healthy lunch and set off for another day at work, checking and double-checking all of the door handles and locks before he left. Smiling to himself almost imperceptibly, he eventually took his seat on the bus.

He felt good today; he ached like an absolute *bitch*, but he felt good.

Arriving at work, he said his usual morning greetings and seated himself at his desk with a grunt; the stiffness in his legs making it painful to sit down at first. That, it seemed, was his first mistake.

"Just pull your chair out further next time, Zach. Or better yet, bring a mattress so you don't have to get up at all." said the girl in the corner, laughing to herself.

"I'm good" he replied, conversationally, "I was out running last night so I'm just a little bit stiff, that's all."

"Yeah. *Sure you were.*" she replied, grinning, and donning her headset.

"I..." he began, but she had already answered her first call of the day.

"U-First Personal Banking; how can I help?" she said, in that whiny, almost musical cadence that human beings only ever seem to use when on the phone. Turning back to his own computer, he let out a long breath.

Here we go again, he thought.

Zach actually didn't mind his job; he knew he wasn't exactly changing the world by working in customer services, but he had always liked talking to people. People who couldn't see him in person, that is. Zach had always felt like a completely different man when he was chatting away to customers on the phone. Here he could be whoever he wanted to be; he could be charming, he could be funny, he could be *thin and attractive* in the minds of those who were not granted the opportunity to see him in the flesh and make the same old snap-judgements based on his physical appearance.

He could be all of those things in *real life*, too, and he was trying.

A few hours passed in the blink of an eye, as they so often do once a person gets in the zone, and Zach logged out of his system to go to lunch. Tupperware tub in hand, he grabbed his water bottle and sought out the break room. He didn't enjoy sitting in there, there were just too many other people around most of the time. Too many other people who stared at him, watched him for any sign of gluttony or otherwise slovenly behaviour, and would chuckle under their breaths, nudging their friends to make sure they, too, caught the show.

It was a regular dance, and one he was tired of.

He opened his lunch box and took out some carrot sticks; definitely not his favourite food, but a necessary evil if he was serious about shifting the weight and making the positive changes he so badly craved. After a few of the carrot sticks, followed by some grapes and an apple, Zach found that he was actually pretty satisfied with his lunch. That was, of course, until one of the other girls came into the break room to make a round of coffees for herself and her friends.

They did not speak to each other, Zach wasn't even sure he knew this girl's name, such was the size of the office and the number of people who worked there.

Charlotte, Charlie? Something like that, he mused.

She walked straight past him to the kitchen worktop and busied herself with cups and spoons. Idly turning to look around the room while the kettle was boiling, she noticed the fruit and vegetables which had constituted his lunch and tried in vain to suppress an involuntary snort of laughter. She turned back around again just as quickly and went to great pains to ensure she did not look directly at him again as she finished her task. With her drinks made and balanced precariously on a tray, she scuttled out of the break room as quickly as she could, sucking at the inside of her own cheeks to keep from grinning too obviously.

In doing so, she did not notice the redness which had started to blossom upon Zach's cheeks, nor the beginnings of tears stirring in his downcast eyes.

He did not wait for nightfall and the cover of darkness but changed into his exercise gear as soon as he got home from work, taking care to fold his suit trousers carefully and place his shoes back inside their box. Once he was ready, he headed out into the street and began to jog with the day's events still at the forefront of his mind.

Within minutes he was sweating and panting, but this discomfort was nothing compared to the abuse he received from the locals.

"Fatty!" shouted one kid.

"Look at this chunky fucker!" shouted another, grinning, and prodding his friend. It wasn't just the neighbourhood kids either, as the middle-aged couple from a few doors down tutted and shook their heads as he jogged past them.

"Watch it, lard-ass!" he heard the husband say under his breath once Zach had passed them. Zach tried to ignore them as he continued apace around the streetlight at the end of the road, then back toward home, passing through the smirking, heckling gauntlet once more.

Once he was back inside, able to rehydrate and bring his heart-rate back down toward what he considered normal, Zach showered in silence and fixed himself an evening salad, with a bowl of mixed nuts waiting for him afterwards: his well-earned treat.

Far from looking forward to this small reward, however, Zach was miserable.

Damned if I do, damned if I don't, he repeated over and over in his head, until he was simply too tired to care either way and took himself upstairs for an early night.

Waking early once more, Zach did not feel motivated to exercise, not one bit. Still, he had started something and meant to see it through. He forced himself to lift his weights and complete a round of push-ups, and once he was moving and his endorphins were willing him on, he decided on a short jog in the early morning cold. More to clear his head than to work his body.

Before long, he was once again on the bus to work with his satchel next to him on the seat. He was all-too aware that he took up more than his fair share of seat, and he hoped that nobody would be forced to try to sit next to him.

He eventually had arrived at work, having resolved on the way to approach today with renewed vigour and just ignore the stifled chuckles and furtive glances.

Upon opening the door to the office, however, it registered somewhere in the back of his mind that it was abnormally quiet despite the usual faces in the usual places. Nevertheless, he proceeded to his desk and pulled his chair out. On doing so, he noticed a folded piece of lined notebook paper. Zach unfolded the note and beheld a crudely drawn, and even more crudely cut-out, picture of a first-prize trophy emblazoned with an 'engraving' which read:

"U-First Personal Banking Olympics.
500m Sprint Winner:
Captain Cupcake"

A split-second later, Zach was practically blinded by the flashes of multiple phone cameras, and a wave of laughter drowned out the sound of the blood pulsing in his ears. Everyone was laughing at him, and many had taken pictures of him holding the 'trophy'.

"That's enough, people; shouldn't you all be logged-on by now?" said the office manager, emerging from his room at the sudden eruption of laughter.

Zach smiled in spite of himself and did as he always did in these situations: said nothing and carried on with his day despite the ton-weight which was threatening to pull his heart down from his chest and into his stomach; maybe even further still, pulling until it was on the floor at his feet just waiting to be stamped on.

Zach did not exercise when he got home after work. He locked the door behind him, closed the curtains, and just sat there in darkness and silence, holding his paper trophy loosely beside him. After about an hour, he turned the living room light on and walked over to the highly polished mantle. He wasn't entirely sure why he did it, but he placed the "Captain Cupcake" trophy front and centre, leaning it against the small carriage clock to keep it upright.

This has to stop. I need to put an end to this. I have to stick up for myself. This has to stop. I need to go on the offensive.

A plan began to coalesce in Zach's mind.

Cupcakes. He thought. *If they want cupcakes, I'll give them fucking cupcakes.*

Zach had always been a fastidious person when it came to his home, if not his body. The rows upon rows of cleaning products and meticulously folded towels bore witness to his dedication. He also liked to stockpile, and had more toilet rolls, cans of beans, and bags of rice stowed away than was really necessary for one man.

He also stockpiled *cupcakes*, just in case. You never know when you might need a good cupcake, especially living alone.

It was to this particular collection he went, first thing the next morning. He felt refreshed and positive having enjoyed a sound, peaceful night's sleep. He selected a bigger bag today, a sports bag as opposed to his usual brown leather satchel.

I need to make sure I can fit all the cupcakes into it, and the sprinkles - can't forget the sprinkles.

He decided to go clean shaven today and placed his best tie around his neck. He splashed on a drop or two of his most expensive aftershave and heaved the bag onto his shoulder before heading off to work as he did every day.

Once seated, Zach placed the sports bag down gently next to him on the bus seat, and hummed a tune under his breath, lost in his thoughts.

This will work... they won't be horrible to me after today. This should work. I've brought enough cupcakes for everybody.

He arrived at work a couple of minutes late - intentionally so he could be sure everyone would be at their desks - and placed the sports bag down on his desk.

He unzipped it and took a deep breath.

"Cupcakes for everyone!" he shouted, reaching into the bag and producing the treats. The first was for the mouthy bitch in the corner, whom he had zero doubt was behind the trophy prank. He walked over to her and gave her the first cake, followed very closely by her friend in the adjacent seat, the giggling girl from the break room.

The first two had been fed, so he turned to feed the rest.

Why are they all screaming? Why are they running away? he wondered. There were more than enough cupcakes to go around, and besides, he had already chained the front and back doors shut to make sure nobody could get out.

Everybody was going to get a cupcake.

Around the office he went, handing out cupcake after cupcake to colleague after colleague. There was one for the team leader who had not stuck up for him. There was one for the manager who only ever came out of his glass-paneled office to shout at them.

He even had one for Kyle, the only one among them who he had thought of as an actual ally, a friend even, but who had laughed just as hard as everybody else when Zach discovered his trophy.

Fifteen frantic minutes later, and it was done.

Everyone had been fed, and all now lay still, bellies full and in need of a good, long sleep.

Zach could hear sirens in the distance, getting closer and closer with each peak and trough of their artificial wail. They would be here any minute.

Luckily, Zach had anticipated this, and had saved the final cupcake for himself.

Delicately picking it up and taking it out of the bag, he put it in his mouth and pulled the trigger.

THE BONE FAIRY

"Will it hurt, Mummy?" asked Cassie, as she nervously tongued the loose tooth.

"Of course not, sweetheart, but we need to pull it otherwise the Tooth Fairy won't come tonight."

Cassie creased her forehead for a moment or two before accepting this display of parental logic with a nod.

"Okay Mummy."

She squeezed her eyes shut in anticipation of inevitable searing agony, but barely even winced as the offending tooth vacated the gum.

"Was that it? That wasn't so bad!" Cassie smiled at her mother.

She had no idea just how bad things were going to get.

Cassie had made sure to brush her remaining teeth thoroughly - *like a good girl* - and was now tucked up tightly in her bed. She checked under her pillow for the third time to make sure her tooth was still there and, upon registering the feel of the soft tissue paper in which the prize was wrapped, she assured herself of its safety once more and turned over, more eager to get to sleep than any child had ever been in the history of planet Earth. Or so it felt to Cassie.

Sleep came quickly and Cassie willingly succumbed to its embrace. With her tooth secure beneath her pillow, she enjoyed one of the soundest night's sleep she could remember. Perhaps unsurprisingly, she awoke earlier than usual the following morning and immediately thrust a hand under her pillow, terrified that the Tooth Fairy had forgotten all about her. In place of the soft tissue paper, Cassie instead felt a cold, hard coin beneath her fingertips. She pulled out the £2 coin and held it up to her eyes in the early morning light.

She came! The Tooth Fairy came! thought an ecstatic Cassie, as she ran into her parents' room to share the wonderful news.

All day at school, Cassie and her friends discussed at length the many and varied delights upon which the Tooth Fairy's £2 could be spent - sweets, magazines, and hair slides being the most popular suggestions.

Cassie sprinted across the playground at 3:30 to her waiting mother. She buckled her seatbelt and they pulled away from the school gates, and in no time at all they had reached the local newsagent.

Sweets, she ultimately decided.

Later that evening, following the excitement of the preceding day, her eyes were heavy as she tried to stave off sleep. Realising it was a losing battle, she kissed her parents goodnight and went upstairs. Cassie went through the usual motions of washing her hands and face, before brushing her teeth and hair. Once she was suitably groomed, she pulled on a fresh pair of pyjamas and climbed into bed.

What a great day, she thought as the warmth of the covers soothed her and carried her inexorably down the path toward sleep. She was exhausted, but her mind was racing with possibilities.

The Tooth Fairy is real! And if the Tooth Fairy is real, there must be other Fairies out there, too!

If you're out there, Fairies, if you can hear me, I wish you could come and visit me every *night.*

For the second night running, Cassie slept heavily and deeply. So soundly did she sleep in fact, that she woke with a groggy, uneasy feeling in her head and a persistent ache in her limbs. She lay a while, trying to bring the room round her into focus. A few minutes later, the details around her began to resolve themselves more fully, and she discerned the usual assortment of toys and decorations in her room. Identifying the mundane seemed to clear her head a little, and she became aware of a new sensation - the rumbling in her stomach which prompted her to climb out of bed.

Breakfast time, she thought.

Swinging her legs to the edge of the bed, Cassie's toes probed around beneath her for the warm comfort of her slippers. Once she had located them, she stepped down from the bed and winced as a lightning bolt of pain issued from her right foot and travelled up her leg.

She placed a steadying hand on the mattress to keep from falling over, then sat back down on her bed. She took her foot in her hand and contorted her leg to bring it up to eye level, expecting to see a drawing pin or craft needle sticking out from her skin. But there was nothing, just her foot. Her furrowed brow betrayed her worry and the feeling, besides her hunger, which was growing in the pit of her stomach; something felt weird, something wasn't right.

She descended the stairs slowly, trying not to place her full weight on the painful right foot, and limping into the kitchen toward her mother.

"What's wrong, sweetheart? Are you okay?" asked Cassie's mum, Caroline.

"My foot hurts," Cassie replied, though the limp had already given the game away somewhat.

"Did you kick something or step on something?" her mother asked sweetly.

"No… I just woke up like this. It hurts, Mummy."

"Well, you don't have school today, so we'll set you up on the sofa or in your bed and you can rest it up, okay?"

An hour or so later, Cassie was once again in her room. The pain in her foot and the worry she felt at its sudden emergence had entirely replaced her hunger, and she merely picked at her toast. She now lay more comfortably on her bed with a book in hand. A pillow elevated her head at one end of the bed, and another held aloft the offending foot at the opposite end.

She woke with a start a little later, not even realising she had fallen asleep in the first place. Her book was now on the floor, the way toast falls butter-side down. Far from feeling refreshed from her relaxing snooze, though, Cassie was troubled by the throbbing pain which persisted in her foot.

"Everything okay, sweetheart?" her mother asked, appearing around the side of her door.

"No… it hurts." Cassie responded meekly, her lip trembling as she blinked away the moisture which had begun to gather in the corners of her eyes.

"Okay, come on, get up; we're going to the hospital."

Fifteen minutes later they were in the car. Cassie's foot was propped up on the back seat as her mother drove to their local A&E.

Once they arrived, Cassie's mother explained the problem to the lady on the front desk and filled in the requisite forms before being instructed to take a seat in the waiting area. However, as is so often the case in English A&E departments, they were not seen too quickly given the low-priority nature of an apparent foot injury. They passed the time as best they could, utilising the magazines and colouring sets provided by the hospital, and waited patiently - more patiently than some - and tried to avoid making eye-contact with the local alcoholic who was presently slurring his way through his weekly demand to *"shpeak to a dog… a dog… a dogta"*.

Around three hours after their arrival, the nurse finally called "Cassie Critchley", and mother and daughter were shown through to the small consultation room. Caroline explained the sudden onset of the pain to the young doctor, who nodded and took notes fastidiously, adding the odd "mm-hmm" along the way. She continued, assuring the young GP that Cassie had not fallen, dropped anything upon, nor otherwise impacted her foot whatsoever. The doctor did not attempt to hide his bewilderment and convened an X-ray. Cassie had never seen such a machine before, and the reassurances of the medical team did little to assuage her fear of the X-ray, *whatever that was*. Ultimately, the X-ray did not hurt Cassie as she had worried it might, and both mother and daughter were sent back to the waiting room to await the results.

They did not have to wait long but were both immediately troubled by the frown lines in the GP's forehead and the tight pursing of his lips. Communicating in gestures alone at this point, the doctor beckoned for the Critchleys to follow him, and shepherded them into their previous seats as he closed the door behind him.

The doctor began.

"Have you ever had any difficulty running or kicking a ball?"
"No."
"Have you visited A&E with aches and pains like this before?"
"No."
"Have you had *any* kind of pain like this before?"
"No."
The quick-fire questions were beginning to grate on Caroline.
"What's going on, doctor? What is it?" she asked sternly, but with a smile which was more for her daughter's benefit than the doctor's.
"Look, here…" the young man said, holding the X-rays up to the light-box on the wall "You see the bones, here? The *metatarsals*, we call them. You see them? Count them."

Realisation dawned on Cassie's mother and her face contorted in confusion.

"There are only four," the doctor confirmed out loud. "Cassie's foot is missing the third metatarsal bone."

The doctor prescribed Cassie some strong painkillers so she would at least feel better physically, if not mentally, and while she did not fully understand the conversation between the doctor and her mother, she understood enough to know that something was wrong.

Her foot was missing a bone! Her foot was missing a bone, and nobody could understand why.

"...so he's going to speak to the specialist first thing on Monday morning, see if she knows what this could be."

Cassie's father, Gavin, nodded as her mother regaled him with the bizarre tale.

"Do they think it's some sort of... wasting disease, something like that?" he asked, just as confused as everybody else.

"We won't know until Monday, but at least she's comfortable now she's got the medication."

They weren't sure whether Cassie could hear their conversation, and they did not want to alarm her any more than she already was, so they quickly changed the subject. The rest of that day, Cassie's parents did what parents of sick children have been doing for generations: waited on her hand and foot and spoiled her rotten.

Despite lying prone on the couch all day, Cassie was exhausted when bedtime eventually rolled around. She had already lost count of the number of Disney movies she'd watched today and was feeling a little sick after devouring almost her entire body weight in ice cream (though she would not tell her parents this). Having received enough tickles and hugs to last a lifetime, she was more than ready to sleep. As per usual, she made quick work of brushing her teeth and washing her face, before changing into her nightwear and crawling into bed.

Thanks to the medication masking the pain in her foot, Cassie managed to fall straight to sleep. Dreams came quickly to her sleeping mind, and the darkness presented Cassie with images of fortified castles and lush rolling hills; of handsome princes and beautiful princesses riding on horseback through enchanted forests. She dreamed of soft, cold ice cream, of colouring books and waiting rooms, of alcoholics and blood-soaked bandages, of red eyes and sharp teeth...

Waking suddenly, Cassie switched on her bedside night-light and cast a panicked look around her bedroom.

Nothing, she thought. *Just a bad dream.*

She slowed her breathing and turned off her night-light, casting the room into darkness once again. She did not check to see what time it was, but instead laid back down and was asleep before her head had even hit the pillow.

The early morning light sneaking in through a break in Cassie's bedroom curtains illuminated the waking girl like a spotlight as she screamed in agony.

Her parents sprinted into her room; eyes wide in terror.

"Mummy! Mummy! My leg!" she screamed as tears streamed down her face, glinting softly in the dawn light. Cassie's father ripped back the bedsheets with the speed and skill of a matador and had to stifle a scream and choke back vomit as he beheld the mangled mass of soft, pulpy flesh which had once been his daughter's lower right leg.

Her mother was not so stoic, however, and yelled out in anguish before immediately covering her mouth with her hands. Gavin Critchley's eyes told his wife to *get a grip,* and he tried to reassure his daughter that she was okay, and everything was going to be fine.

"Get her pills and call an ambulance!" he instructed his wife, who followed his instructions to the letter. Hoping the drugs would ease Cassie's pain until the ambulance arrived, Gavin tentatively probed his daughter's lower leg and met little to no resistance, as if the shin bone itself was missing.

The ambulance arrived in short order, and the paramedics - despite their obvious alarm and confusion - stowed Cassie safely aboard and placed a mask over her face to better administer their more potent brand of pain relief.

A little while later, a doctor sought out Cassie's parents and found them in the waiting room to deliver his initial verdict. It seemed to Caroline and Gavin that they had been waiting there for an eternity, but it was really only an hour or so after they had left the family home in the speeding ambulance.

"Mr. and Mrs. Critchley? Okay, well Cassie is asleep and for now she's comfortable - that's the main thing. But I have to ask… What happened?"

"Aren't *you* supposed to be telling *us* that?!" Caroline shouted at the doctor.

"Mrs. Critchley, you have to understand; we've never seen anything like this before. *Ever.* From what you told the paramedics, your daughter woke early this morning missing her entire tibia and fibula, and according to her file, she lost a whole metatarsal just the night before. What's more, I cannot find a single incision, scar, stitch nor hole which might suggest a surgical removal. That's just not possible."

The three simply stood looking at each other for a long moment.

"Are you accusing us of something, doctor?" asked Cassie's father, trying his best to keep a lid on his anger.

"No, no, Mr. Critchley, no. It's not for me to insinuate anything, I just need all the facts so I can make the correct diagnosis, that's all. As I said, she's sleeping, but you can go in and see her now if you would like."

The doctor left them alone with their daughter while he went to make the necessary calls and arrangements. He scheduled the inevitable raft of tests which would hopefully discern exactly what sort of syndrome, disease, or pathogen they could possibly be dealing with here.

What could simply erase entire bones from the human body overnight? he thought as he went about his work.

Cassie's parents sat by her bedside but did not speak as they stared at their little girl with tears in their eyes.

What's happening to her? What the fuck is going on? they thought as one.

Cassie slept the artificial sleep of the hospitalised and medicated while her parents looked on with concern and confusion etched onto their faces as if carved by a stone mason. As the doctors and nurses came and went to check in on their daughter, administer her medication, and carry out a plethora of tests, the most perfunctory of pleasantries were exchanged by all.

Caroline and Gavin talked around in circles for hours regarding the possible cause of their little girl's baffling ailment.

Could it be something we've given her to eat? they wondered.

Does one of us have a faulty gene we're unaware of? they considered.

Is this our fault?

They eventually accepted the nurse's offer of pillows and blankets and tried to sleep as best they could in the uncomfortable chairs beside Cassie's bed, and the trauma of the day's events soon put paid to their waking minds. Husband and wife alike drifted effortlessly into a deep slumber, undisturbed by the frequent visits from the ever-attentive medical team.

The windows had long since grown dark with the setting of the sun, and the night had truly wrapped its cold fingers around the small hospital room in which mother, father, and daughter slept. The electronic displays and blinking LEDs of life-saving machinery were now the only illumination to be found.

As Cassie's parents slept, their minds began to fill with dark and disturbing images: a bone here, a vein there, a harsh plastic tube and a soft, delicate throat. A syringe pierces skin as a bone breaks somewhere off in the endless darkness, unseen but undoubtedly heard.

Cassie's dreams were filled with far worse than the uncomfortable medical iconography conjured up by the mind of a traumatised parent. Her subconscious screamed at her while her body lay still and silent.

Teeth. She saw teeth. And eyes, too. Glowing, red eyes. She heard a mirthless, mocking laugh, a scornful snicker, full of disdain.

It can't be human, Cassie thought.

Then a voice; a snatched, distant snippet of a voice in her mind, mocking her, taunting her from some unseen corner of her psyche.

Visit you every night…

Cassie's screams, muffled as they were by the mask over her mouth and nose, instantly woke her parents, and caused the doctor and nurses to run into the room with a practiced urgency. The medical team shooed the panicked parents out of the room and rushed to the aid of the girl, who was screaming through her tears and clutching wildly at her torso.

The doctor wasted no time in sedating Cassie so he could work. He performed a thorough examination of the girl, paying particular attention to the area of her chest she had been clutching so tightly. His hands and fingers massaged and probed the area, and his black hair swayed back and forth as he shook his head in utter bewilderment.

"No, no, no…. No, it can't be. No, no… Nurse - X-ray, now!"

Once the X-ray had been taken, the doctor made his way to a private room and closed the door, ignoring the pleas and appeals of the Critchleys. He stood staring in wonder at the black and white image he held in his shaking hands.

The third metatarsal… the fibula and tibia… now this? Impossible… just fucking impossible.

Once he had assured himself that there had been no mistake made by his staff nor irregularity thrown up by his equipment, the doctor resolved to seek out the girl's parents. A few minutes later, he was seated across from the distressed Critchley's in his own consultation room, and the X-ray lay conspicuously on the table between them. Gavin and Caroline were already at the end of their respective tethers with all of this, so were only vaguely cognizant of words like "intercostal", "clavicular", and "xiphoid" before they had heard quite enough.

"What are you saying, doctor? Speak fucking English, man."

The doctor took a second to swallow down his own frustration and catch a calming breath, then repeated his findings as plainly as he could.

"What I'm saying, Mr. Critchley - Gavin - is that your daughter has woken up missing two of her rib bones."

Cassie was moved almost immediately to the Intensive Care ward, though the doctors still had no idea what was causing her sudden and horrific bone loss. Over the course of the day, orthopedic specialists came and looked at her, followed by a seemingly endless queue of endocrinologists, rheumatologists, and physiatrists. Not one among them could fathom with any degree of certainty the cause of Cassie's unique condition.

Her parents were forced to wait on the sidelines, not permitted into the ICU, instead being asked to remain in the family room and await round the clock updates.

Cassie was still sedated, and her enforced sleep was very much for her own benefit, or so the doctors reasoned. The machines which encircled her and the plastic tubes which protruded so unnaturally from her arms and nostrils were necessary but had so far done little to remedy her situation.

Doctors and specialists of all disciplines had performed their tests, made their notes, consulted with their peers, and had long since retired for the night leaving Cassie's care to the night shift team who visited Cassie, checked her, medicated her, and logged their findings with a staggering frequency. The ICU was nothing if not efficient

The morning was fast approaching but the outside world was still in darkness. A young nurse checked her watch and confirmed it was 4am: time to check on Cassie. She made to stand up from her desk and swooned with a dizziness and fatigue that she had had no cause to anticipate. She sat back down, just for a moment.

The young nurse was startled awake by a scream which curdled the very lifeblood of all within earshot, and she was mortified by a glance at her watch which now read 4:17.

She had fallen asleep and slept for nearly twenty minutes.

The scream rang out once more.

Cassie!

The nurse raced into the girl's room alongside three other medical staff and yelled in terror as she beheld the child, screaming in agony in her bed. She instinctively held her hands out toward the poor girl, but Cassie did not - could not - reach back.

Beneath each of her small, round shoulders, were long strips of pink and purple flesh, terminating in mangled balls of skin and vein.

With agonising guilt coursing through her own veins, the nurse registered absently that those must have been the girl's arms and hands, once.

Cassie's remarkable tale had somehow gotten out of the hospital and into the hands of the media, and the hospital's security personnel were hard at work keeping the snooping, unconscionable reporters at bay.

The local hospital could no longer hope to deal with - let alone contain or prevent - whatever it was which was so rapidly and so devastatingly ailing Cassie, so preparations were now under way for her to be airlifted to a major city hospital in a neighbouring county.

Her parents were now at home, frantically packing cases and shoulder bags with shaking hands and swollen, exhausted eyes. The news that Cassie had now lost both arms and both hands overnight to this *thing* had knocked the very steam out of both Caroline and Gavin, who were leaning on each other both literally and figuratively. So raw were their emotions and so fraught were their nerves, they were struggling to keep their heads above water.

Cassie had not been fully awake for days at this point, not since she had lost her lower leg, in fact. Her medically induced sleep was a torrid, frightful cage from which she had no agency to escape. Pain, fear, foreboding, terror: these were Cassie's companions now.

And the voice.

Visit you every *night,* it mocked, the sound of the words like a fly scratching against her eardrum. It laughed a merciless laugh, and Cassie once again tried in vain to scream.

Visit you every *night… to feed. For feed, we must… Visit you every night, until there is nothing left to feed upon…*

The red eyes, the teeth, the horrendous cackle, these were Cassie's entire world. The knowledge pressed down hard on her broken body, until a cold wave of relief flooded through her as the medication was administered to her. She drifted behind her consciousness, away from the pain, and away from the cackling, demonic creature which had so badly plagued her dreams of late.

That night, Cassie felt different. She felt as though she had been turned around, as if she were somewhere else.

In a different bed? she correctly speculated, since the air ambulance had indeed transferred her successfully to the huge city hospital where a whole new team of doctors and nurses were now responsible for her care.

Cassie was once again medicated and unconscious. She hoped deep down that the feeling of weightlessness, the sensation of floating she had experienced earlier meant that she had now outrun the creature. She lay there inside the darkness of her own mind, with only her thoughts for company.

Only my thoughts, she realised. *No voice, no eyes, no laughing.*

There she lay. For how long, she could not tell. But she was alone, she knew that much.

Slowly, the shape of the room in which she lay began to come into focus. At first, the blinking LEDs on the machinery around her hurt her eyes, and she couldn't actually remember the last time she had opened them.

Why now? she thought. *Why am I waking up now?*

As if in answer, her right foot, right leg, ribcage and both arms announced themselves in blinding, white-hot pain, and Cassie came fully awake for the first time in days. She looked around in a panic for a doctor, a nurse, her Mummy, or anyone to come and help her, and was as confused as she was terrified at the sight she beheld. Ten, maybe eleven people were slumped over their desks, laid on the floor, or were propped at bizarre angles against the wall.

I make them sleep, Cassie... I make them all *sleep.*

This time Cassie did not scream, so overcome with terror that it rooted her in place and froze her mouth tightly shut. She could not discern the direction from which the voice was coming; it seemed to be coming from everywhere and nowhere all at once.

They sleep, I feast... they sleep, I feast.

I feast, you die.

And then she saw it, crouched and coiled in the corner of her hospital room, half-hidden in the darkness, and chewing on what she could only assume to be one of her own bones.

A fairy, she realised.

The creature cast aside the humerus upon which it had been gnawing and stared at Cassie with glowing red eyes and razor-sharp teeth gleaming in a wide, cruel smile. It remained still and grinning for a further few seconds, and Cassie could hardly breathe as she met its unnatural gaze. Suddenly, it leapt up onto the foot of her bed and crawled slowly towards her face with its mouth wide open.

I feast, you die! I feast, you die!

This time Cassie *did* scream, but only for a moment.

CHILDREN OF THE MOUNTAIN

They could only move at night, under the cover of darkness. The light brought innumerable dangers, and the risk to the party was simply too great to warrant venturing out while it held sway. They had set out as a group of five, yet only two now remained. The light brought the creatures, the Trolls. Huge, lumbering behemoths of questionable intelligence, yet they constituted a grave threat to Hakko, Q'San, and all of their kind.

Worse than the Trolls, though, was their *machine*. What it actually was, Hakko and Q'San could only guess at. Was it transport of some kind, a harvester, or a tool of war, death, and chaos? One thing they did know for certain, though, was that it came with the light. Once day had fully broken, the machine would come for them, as it had come for so many of their kind over the long years.

The rumble served as the first warning. The low, dull vibration which started as an indistinct tremor until the very ground shook beneath their feet heralded the approach of the machine as surely as a blown horn or a rung bell might. Then came the sound, the deafening *whoosh* as the vehicle began its daily rounds of indiscriminate killing in service of the giant Trolls.

"We must get back to The Mountain," Hakko clicked in his native tongue to Q'San, his only surviving companion. They had descended The Mountain days earlier, leaving the safety of their cave behind in order to seek out food for their nest-mates and hatchlings. Hakko had known that this journey was already going to be a perilous enough affair in and of itself, and the added complication of the creatures and their machine only served to further fuel his anxieties.

Hakko and his kin had heard the tales and the songs which lamented the Trolls and their tool of destruction since they were but mere hatchlings themselves, but they had never encountered these mythical icons until they had embarked upon this fateful expedition, which had already cost the lives of three of their number.

So far, thought Hakko without a hint of sarcasm or irony.

"I agree, Hakko, but the light persists. You know the perils," replied Q'San, his own mandibles quivering as he pleaded with his old friend. Q'San was younger than his companion by a number of cycles, and he was already exhausted by the events of their quest, but he was also just as eager as his friend to reach The Mountain and the safety it promised. The machine stayed on the ground; it could not reach the summit of The Mountain to which they so desperately sought a swift return. They had a plan, but still had a long way to go. At length, the pair agreed that nothing further could - or rather *should* - be done until the darkness came once more to offer what scant sanctuary it could, and so they instead set about finding such shelter as was available and hunkered down.

There's no wind here, thought Hakko, absently.
Once we passed through The Arch and into the Trolls' realm, the wind stopped. He made a mental note of this bizarre fact and woke

Q'San from his sleep, the darkness having fallen, and the Trolls now dispersed. *No wind, no sound, no rumble.*

No machine.

Hakko and Q'San's people did not have one single, definitive name for the strange planet on which they lived and died; they just thought of it as *home*. Had they evolved here, or were they originally visitors to this world who had lain roots and thrived for centuries or more? If the truth of this existential query was known to any of their kind, Hakko and Q'San were not counted among their number.

Forcing this abstract and currently pointless rumination from his thoughts, Hakko considered their next move.

"We have a great distance to cover before the light returns, my friend," he said to a now awake and alert Q'San.

"… and the journey will not be easy".

Leaving the safety of their shelter and taking their first tentative steps into the darkness, their every sense was alert for any possible signs of danger. Thankfully, the terrain here was not too difficult to negotiate, soft and dry as grass, the hue a deep grey in the darkness. Not difficult, then, but vast, nonetheless.

Across this plain they trekked, picking up speed and making good time, when Q'San suddenly stopped in his tracks and held his breath, his younger, keener eyes alert to some unknown shape in the distance. Cautiously, carefully, the travelers crept toward this unknown object until it resolved itself before them.

Food, Hakko discerned, *but not for us.*

One of the many reasons Hakko's kind had never knowingly sought out the company of the Trolls was their wastefulness. The clumsy, brainless, uncouth creatures were as ambivalent about their food supplies as they were to the killing of those they deemed *lesser beings*. It was not uncommon for expeditionary parties such as Hakko and Q'San's to stumble across piles of discarded food which the bumbling Trolls had either knowingly cast aside, or absent-mindedly dropped in their haste and carelessness.

Arrogant fools, he thought.

We starve in our caves and must watch our nest-mates die. Those few hundred hatchlings which do happen to reach maturity each cycle - through sheer force of will and the sacrifice of their kin - do so as emaciated and sickly creatures. Yet these Trolls casually throw away such sustenance as even the fabled greed of their kind could not accommodate.

The food was dry and stale, devoid of any nutrients which Hakko's kind could partake. It may as well have been a rock, for all the good it would do them.

We are hunters, he thought angrily. *We set our traps and ensnare our prey. Those which skitter and scuttle beneath our feet are our food, not this dehydrated mass before us. The cowardly ones who take to the skies upon buzzing wings - those are our food. Yet they are a rare sight indeed in these lands. As if they, too, fear the Trolls.*

Hakko exchanged a knowing glance with his friend, and they moved on, dejected at the reminder of the stupidity displayed by the inhabitants of this bizarre realm. It served as a stark reminder of the dire nature of their own predicament.

They forged on, making progress across this vast land despite the darkness which lay heavily around them and bore down upon them. This was indeed their first journey into the Troll realm, but they had been raised on the tales of those few, legendary heroes of cycles past who had survived their own quests and returned to the safety of the cave high upon the peak of The Mountain. These songs and tales were at the forefront of their minds as they forged ahead, so even though they knew it was coming, the sudden change in the terrain still served to shock them, so stark was the contrast.

They had reached *The Hard Lands*.

The way back home would not be a mere retracing of their initial incursion; the journey home was to be via an alternate path to maximise their chances of finding food for their nest-mates and hatchlings.

The soft, grass-like terrain gave way to a hard, unyielding, slippery expanse, as if it were a lake frozen over by the winter cold.

Except it isn't cold here, thought Hakko, *and there's no wind*.

As they made their way forwards on this treacherous leg of their return-journey, they were struck by just how much of the Trolls' food was scattered about these lands, inedible as it may be to their kind. The pair pressed on, adjusting to the hard ground despite the pains and twinges it elicited in their sore, tired legs.

"Hakko" said Q'San wearily, "I have to stop, I need to rest."

Hakko stopped beside his friend and cast a look around them, assessing their current location and circumstances. He agreed with Q'San, and the duo once more began to search for what little shelter they could find in this hard, harsh environment. Once they had satisfied themselves that their chosen location was indeed the best they were going to get out here, they dug in. They were at least shielded from sight in the nook they had discovered, which was all they could really hope for in reality.

Yes, this will have to do, thought Hakko.
It's starting to get light anyway.

Hakko woke with a start, panic and dread filling him as he regained his focus and awareness of his surroundings.

"Q'San! Wake up, quickly! We were too long in our slumber, they are here!"

Q'San was suddenly as awake and alert as his leader, and he dared to peer out from behind their makeshift shelter. He could see the lands beyond in all their strange glory, the light having returned to bathe the world in its harsh glory once more.

"We have to move!" he said to Hakko, "We cannot stay here!"

"No, my friend, we're too exposed. We'd be risking everything were we to be reckless in our actions; patience is our ally here!" Hakko reasoned with his young companion.

But Q'San had already made up his mind.

"No, my friend, I cannot stay here. I grow wearier and wearier by the hour; I have a hunger which I cannot sate. I must take this chance!" he moved as if to leave but Hakko restrained him.

"Don't be foolish! Think about the hatchlings!" he said to his friend in an attempt to show him the folly of his brashness.

"I *am* thinking about the hatchlings," Q'San replied stoically. "I'm sorry. I have to go, and now. It is light, yes, but there is no sign of the Trolls yet."

Q'San fixed Hakko with a long, meaningful stare, one full of love and hope. But also one of determination.

"Wish me luck, old friend."

Pulling free of Hakko's restraining grasp, which had loosened in the face of his young companion's resolve, Q'San burst from their hiding spot and out onto the hard terrain at a full run.

He appeared to be making good progress, and Hakko wondered if a little of Q'San's recklessness was indeed going to be necessary after all, if the pair were to fulfil their mission where so many before them had failed. Hakko was deep in thought, contemplating whether or not to follow his friend out onto the land beyond when a deep rumble interrupted his musings and brought his attention snapping back to the here and now.

No… no, no, no… he thought.

The rumble intensified and the noise came at last. A great, blaring cacophony which heralded the arrival of a huge, lumbering Troll. Before him, he pushed the great machine which had so long been the nemesis of Hakko's kind - a closed door which had halted their ascendancy for generations; a punctuation mark which had so callously ended their collective tale.

Q'San was caught far from the safety of his former hiding spot and was helpless as the machine ploughed into him - or rather *over* him. His limbs were torn asunder as his bright light was extinguished by the might of this insurmountable weapon.

Hakko could only look on in horror and despair as his friend - the fourth on this quest - was killed by the Trolls.

At least he no longer suffers, thought a devastated Hakko.

He hunkered down once again behind the shelter to which he had so tightly clung as his friend was decimated before his eyes.

Once the light has gone and the darkness returns, I will continue. Alone.

Hakko was determined to keep his mind clear and calm. It would not do to dwell on his pain at this point, when so much depended on him. He knew he would need all of his strength and courage if he was going to complete his mission, and he tried to formulate a plan as the light faded and the darkness crept in once again.

The coast was now clear, and the darkness was deafening in its silence. Hakko set to work on his traps, weaving his snares intricately between carefully selected structures. All the while he disguised his own presence with the skill of a master hunter, and he waited for some unwitting creature to stumble blindly into his lure.

He did not have to wait long.

The tell-tale *hum* of vibrating wings which his kind knew so well kindled a hope inside of him, a hope that all might not be lost after all, that his friends may yet be vindicated in their sacrifices.

I cannot abide those filthy beasts, he thought, ironically. In life they disgusted him, but in death they nourished him.

The trap was sprung within mere moments of Hakko registering the humming sound, as the winged beast flew headlong into his snare. The creature was stuck fast and going nowhere, so Hakko pounced, sinking his teeth into the creature and paralysing it where it lay. He wasted no time as he drank deep of his victim, replenishing his own vitality while leeching that of his unwitting prey.

Once he had taken as much nourishment as he dared, Hakko bound the creature tight, careful to keep it alive for now. He found that his strength was returning now, thanks to his much-needed meal. He was reinvigorated as he set off into the darkness, dragging the hapless creature behind him.

His quarry was slowing him down despite his renewed vigor, but Hakko made it to the borders of The Hard Lands whilst the darkness still held sway. He resolved to journey onwards as long as his tired body would allow, so he pushed on inexorably forward toward The Mountain.

At length he found himself back on the soft grasses once more, where the going was easier than it had been on the slippery, solid plains. He forged ahead with the food for his nest-mates and hatchlings in tow, still bound and paralysed ready to be devoured in the feast that would no doubt be held in his honour upon his return to the caves.

On and on he pressed until the darkness began to thin and stray rays of light broke through the canopy. *Not far...keep going,* he told himself, meaning to reach the foot of The Mountain before the light reached its peak and exposed him. He redoubled his efforts and increased his pace as the winged creature bounced along behind him as it was dragged ever more quickly toward the sanctuary of The Mountain's shadow.

I must reach The Mountain. I must reach The Mountain, he repeated over and over in his mind.

And reach it, he eventually did.

Now for the difficult part, Hakko thought.

Everything which had transpired thus far - the hunger, the exhaustion, the loss of his friends - paled into insignificance compared to the sheer scale of the task now at hand. The Mountain was unfathomably tall, and as Hakko looked upwards his eyestalks strained in pain, yet he could still not discern its peak.

One thing at a time, he rationalised, to keep the desperation at bay.

He scouted and searched the area at the foot of The Mountain, meaning to discover a nook in which to ensconce both himself and his prize while he once again settled in to wait out the increasingly ubiquitous light. He found a suitable crevasse with little difficulty and waited.

From his spot beneath The Mountain he could see, hear, and feel the comings and goings of the Trolls and their dreaded machine, at least as long as the light held. He gave in neither to temptation nor impatience, but instead held fast and waited them out. He had his prize, and he had reached his destination.

Not long, he thought, *wait but a little longer my hatchlings, and this feast will be yours.*

When the darkness returned and the lands were once again silent, he secured the bound creature and emerged, determined, from his nook. There was only one thing for it: he had to climb.

He struggled at first to generate any meaningful momentum, but he soon found that he was climbing with some semblance of pace and rhythm. Up and up he climbed, plunder in tow, until he could climb no longer. He came to a stop on a mesa, a natural stair on the face of The Mountain, upon which he could rest a moment. As he regained his energy, he reflected on the tribulations that this journey had cast in his way and was encouraged to think he had come so far. He allowed himself a moment to think of Q'San and the others before getting back on his feet and taking up the climb once again.

Hours passed and Hakko's climb continued in earnest. He had allowed himself that one single break but could ill-afford to do so again as the light would soon return bringing danger with it. Although the Trolls and their machine never ventured beyond the surface lands and certainly never climbed The Mountain, Hakko felt certain that the coming of the light would invite other threats should he be caught out here on The Mountain's face.

Up and up he climbed, fatigued, hungry, and the first green shoots of doubt and despair began to sprout from somewhere deep within him. He swallowed these fears down as best as he could and climbed on, with the unconscious beast still bound and dragging behind him.

Finally, after what seemed an age to Hakko, he reached the top of The Mountain and slumped down in exhaustion. As he regained his feet, he noticed that the light was now at its apex and this revelation served to snap him back to attention. He drew on his deepest reserves of strength to forge ahead. His cave, his hatchlings, his very *salvation* were now within range.

RUMBLE...

The very ground shook beneath Hakko's feet, and his gaze darted left and right in panic. Then came the noise.

Suddenly, as if materialising from nowhere, a Troll strode clumsily toward Hakko. A Troll in whose possession was *the machine.*

No.... no! It cannot be!! How is it here?! The machine! How did it get up here? How did it get to the top of The Mountain? What kind of witchcraft is this?!

Hakko could no longer hold back the rising tides of panic and desperation, not when he had come so far and lost so much. He decided to take the only course of action left to him.

For the pain he had endured, for the friends had he lost, he unslung the hapless creature at his back and ran. He could now see the cave entrance in the distance, practically calling his name, inviting him, willing him home, but the rumble and the sound of the machine were drawing ever closer.

On he ran, every part of him screaming with a heady mix of fear and adrenaline.

On he ran, but he could feel the pull of the mighty device's gravity as it slowed his sprint, pulling him in, dragging him inexorably backwards and toward its gaping maw.

He struggled against the pull with all the strength of his ancestors coursing through him, but with a *pop* he lost the battle and was pulled upwards into the colossal machine.

His body was broken, and he was dragged spinning upwards into the void as the light faded from his eyes and the life ebbed from his pulverised body.

One final thought flashed through Hakko's mind as he succumbed to the eternal nothingness of death.

"I failed. I failed my hatchlings."

·····

Gary barely even registered the spider which he'd just sucked up into his Dyson, and simply continued on with the cleaning, meaning to finish before his wife got home from work.

Besides, the upstairs *had* been badly in need of a good hoovering.

FILM NOIRE

It's important that she lay completely still, not moving a muscle, or she'll ruin it. She'll ruin the art. It's all about the shape, you see, the pattern, the landscape her body creates.

I move my camera in concert with her lines and her curves, focusing in on the light and the shadow in turn. The light illuminates the imperfections, the darkness emphasises the beauty hidden beyond.

This is not photography though; photographers are cunts - almost as bad as fucking poets. *No, this is film. There is nothing to be gained, no benefit whatsoever in capturing a still frame, a lifeless snapshot of a moment. There is nothing in freezing the beauty, embalming it, much less trying to describe it in fucking rhyming couplets when whole seconds, minutes, and hours of nuance can be captured on film.*

No, film is pure.

And so is she.

Her name is Noire, and she lies here unmoving as I film her.

Many so-called "purists" believe that artificial light is an abomination, a poor substitute for natural sunlight.

Bullshit.

Artificial, electric light is just as good, if not better than "real" light - for one thing it allows me to work at night. So here I am, pointing my huge, bright stage light at...

"No! Not like that, here... Let me..."

An errant strand of hair. It had to be moved, and moved by me. I'm the one with the fucking camera, not her. I'm the one with the camera and the one with the vision.

Would you trust a dog to tie its own lead? Would you let a pig slaughter itself? Of course not, so I'll be the one who makes the fucking adjustments, okay?

For fuck sake.

Anyway, where was I?

Oh yes, the light... No, I've lost my train of thought now. That fucking bitch *made me lose my train of thought.*

Another position, another angle.

A chance to alter my vision a little. Noire is lying on her front now, and naked. I dim the lights so that the whole scene is diffused with... uncertainty. Her finer details are difficult to make out at any more than three or four feet in this light. As I zoom in and focus the camera on her back, it's more important than ever that she lay completely fucking still.

I am zoomed in close now. I move the camera from the dimples at the base of her spine, up her back, toward her shoulders. I linger on her shoulder blades for a few moments, my hands stoic and unmoving as the lens captures the light and shadows cast by the shape of bone under her pale skin.

The only natural light which actually succeeds in penetrating the lazy darkness of this room is now moving slowly across her, moonlight moving as sunlight rolls across an open plain. A meadow. A killing field.

Her hair is lit unexpectedly by this stray moonlight and falls casually to the left as she tilts her head a fraction.

No. No, that won't do. That won't do at all.

"What the fuck are you doing? Are you trying to sabotage me? You know how important my vision is! What the fuck is your problem?"

Of course she doesn't answer, she knows she has to stay still.

Another change of position for Noire and a change of film for me. I remove the full reel from my camera. It's an old-school movie-making camera, vintage, not one of those modern, digital monstrosities. I would never *debase myself filming with a fucking - I can barely even bring myself to say it -* mobile phone.

The reel is changed, and the lighting is reset. Noire is suitably posed and we continue filming. I start with her face this time: her eyes closed and her countenance betraying no signs of emotion.

Good.

I need her to be still.

Moving down now, I circle around behind once more to capture the back of her neck and shoulders, before sweeping back around to the front to linger momentarily on her breasts. Her small, pert mounds glisten in the moonlight, and I am reminded that she is barely nineteen years old. I move on slowly once again, and the camera focuses on her flat, toned stomach as I zoom ever-so-slightly to focus the lens on her belly button.

Lower still I go, and the camera now registers - as I do - that her legs are parted suggestively, and I accept her unspoken invitation to explore the regions beyond. The movement of the camera slows to a silent crawl as I zoom in and refocus on her forbidden areas.

I go higher now, past her stomach to encapsulate her ribs. I briefly pause once again on her breasts - so enticing I find them - before moving on to my final shot.

I capture her collarbone, so pronounced between her slight shoulders, and now indelibly recreated in my lens and upon my film. I move to take in the natural cavity at the base of her throat, before finally moving higher still, to frame the angry, red, jagged maw from which her lifeblood had spilled so freely when I slit her throat earlier this afternoon.

She is so still.

I need her to be still.

Before today she had lain still out of fear.

Fear and memory.

Fear of what I would *do to her, and memory of what I* had *done to her.*

Now, though, her stillness is absolute as she lies in the clutches of rigor.

Noire… Her name is Noire.

And my name is Dorian.

Noire and Dorian, can you believe our names?

Our parents were pretentious cunts. 'Artsy-fartsy' types. Hippies, really, before they died.

Our parents.
I filmed them, too.

IN THE UNDERGROWTH

Why is it always dog walkers?

Think about it; It's never the early morning runners. It's never the shady, under-cover-of-darkness fly-tippers, nor is it ever those infernal, wandering Jesus-freaks who are so hell-bent on forcing their beliefs on everybody else that they often blink and miss their entire lives.

No, it's always *the fucking dog walkers.*

So there I was, walking my dog…

*

Nothing particularly interesting had ever really happened to Alan. Firstly, his name was *Alan* for Christ's sake - how many thirty-five-year-olds do you know named Alan?

Perpetually single, working a dead-end office job so mind-numbingly uninspiring that its finer details warrant no further attention here, he was just sort of *plodding* through life, blissfully unaware of the many and varied wonders and opportunities that existed out there in the wider world should he design to simply raise his head above the parapet and actually take a risk every now and then. In short, Alan was just a fucking *loser*, one who lived well and truly inside his own head, eschewing friendships and potential romances for the simple pleasures of locking his doors and opening his well-stocked drinks cabinet. Alan was teetering on the brink of alcoholism and was already in the iron grip of depression, though he didn't necessarily acknowledge this, at least not consciously.

Is there anything worse than a Monday morning? Alan had already sent his boss a text message to say he was going to have to take a sick day, shamelessly and falsely reporting the mother of all stomach-based catastrophes, so he turned straight back over and fell back into a hazy, dreamless sleep.

He awoke suddenly just after 9am to find that his head still swam in the death throes of a two-day hangover, and his mouth felt like he'd swallowed sand in place of wine - his *true* sickness. A little later having drank two hastily arranged and less than adequately prepared coffees and dutifully fed his dog, a small, unassuming terrier he had named "Kratos", Alan threw on a pair of jogging bottoms and a slightly stained hoodie and set off to take the dog on its morning walk. With Kratos in tow and his ear phones firmly in place, he set off for what he had intended to be a quick, ten minute walk which, if he was honest with himself, was more for the sake of his own fragile, aching body than for little Kratos' benefit.

He's only a dog, fuck him, Alan thought chuckling. He didn't mean it of course, he was actually pretty attached to that little shit. Despite his many and varied personal struggles, one thing Alan *did* have going for him was his living situation; his house wasn't anything to shout about - two bedrooms and a reasonably sized garden for the dog to play in - but at least he was out in the countryside where bars, shops, taxis, and teenagers were not the order of the day, but fields, trees, railway tracks and most importantly, relative silence.

He was lost once more in the confines of his own thoughts, his mind dwelling on nothing and everything at once and already a good twenty or so minutes into their journey before Alan had the almost abstract and thoroughly uninteresting realisation that he was a bit lost. Well, not *lost* exactly, but he had certainly walked beyond the turning Kratos and he usually took on their walk which had been committed to muscle-memory at this point. This fact snapped him out of his revelry and he made the decision to just keep going in this direction to see where it led.

Who knows, there may be a huge pot of money, drugs, or both at the end of this overgrown, unkempt country lane, he thought sarcastically.

Alan stopped to give Kratos a quick drink and took one himself from a second bottle he'd brought along for the hangover. They proceeded at a slower pace given the uneven ground, the dense foliage, and the generally forgotten nature of this particular part of the world.

His mind was still clouded and his music was still blaring, and Alan began to look upon this more as an adventure than an accidental detour. His alcohol-addled brain imagined he was Frodo Baggins, and Kratos was the world's worst Samwise Gamgee. On they went with no real direction nor purpose in mind until they happened upon a roughly person-sized tear in a wire mesh fence. His brows narrowed slightly in wonder as to what could possibly lay beyond this de facto portal, and the hungover Alan made a decision which a sober Alan probably would not.

He squeezed through the fence with some difficulty and helped his dog through after him, and the duo set off at a much slower pace than was truly necessary. Something felt a bit *off* to Alan. The foliage reeked of the damp, the weeds were nearly as tall as Alan himself, and the area was littered with all manner of decaying plants and grasses. On they pressed with their hackles inexplicably up when Alan abruptly pulled the earphones out from under his hood and stood stock-still. He had never personally experienced it before but knew immediately what it was from all of those police shows and true crime documentaries he watched at night with bottle of wine in hand and Kratos asleep soundly at his feet.

That smell; that sweet yet sickly, thick, overwhelming smell he could almost taste. That unusual, cloying smell could mean only one thing.

Alan stood in place with his hands on his head and simply swore out loud for what seemed hours rather than seconds, his legs leaden and rooted to the spot with the dawning reality weighing firmly down upon him.

At length, remembering the noble hero character he had absent-mindedly created for himself during this adventure of Kratos and his, he decided to forge ahead. After securely tying the dog's lead to the nearest tree, Alan took a deep breath; rather he tried to, but he gagged and choked on the smell which now permeated his every sense. He jumped up and down on the spot a few times whilst simultaneously shaking his hands in an attempt to psych himself up and get the blood flowing again, before he took a few tentative steps into the unknown.

The whole world seemed to have been shrunken down to a few square metres and was slowly being unveiled to Alan incrementally with each new step he took. Countries, governments, football matches, video games; the world he knew had disappeared in an instant and now there existed only his legs, his senses, and his direction of travel.

The silence screamed in his ears and his stomach threatened to empty with each movement he made, and he eventually discovered the source of the smell. The sight he beheld elicited within him twenty different emotions within a blink of an eye.

"It must've been red at some point."

Why he said this out loud, he never quite figured out. But there, half-buried by the overgrown and positively menacing greenery was a damp, soiled, barely recognisable rolled up carpet; a carpet which must have been a vibrant red at some point, its elaborate patterns long since lost to the elements.

His judgement was still slightly clouded by the previous night's drinks, and Alan permitted himself a closer look as he gingerly moved away some of the foliage with his foot. Jutting out from the top of the carpet and hitherto unseen was a ghostly white, soggy, utterly inhuman hand and wrist.

But it *was* human, human and very much dead.

That was enough. Hungover or not, role-playing a legendary hero or not, Alan threw up. Once he had heaved free the contents of his stomach until his throat was raw, a new wave of emotion came over Alan and he, very deliberately and with a strange grace, sat on the ground and cried.

A few minutes later, vaguely aware of Kratos' whimpers from somewhere behind him, a strange look came over Alan's face as a thought crossed his mind.

"One look... just one quick look" he said, again, out loud "...then I'll call the police"

He stood once more and again used his foot to gently kick open the de facto cocoon, tempting it to spill its ghastly contents.

And spill it did. Almost as if it were part of a macabre children's game, the carpet rolled and unfolded, and out onto the rotten, dirty ground poured a rotten, dirty corpse.

The smell which had so offended Alan earlier - how long ago? How long had he been here? He could not say - now multiplied a hundred-fold and he retched and hacked what little bile his now empty stomach would yield until the moment passed and he had composed himself once more.

A woman, or something vaguely resembling a woman at least. He could see her long hair, could make out the unmistakeable shape of breasts protruding through a stained grey vest, and what he believed to be black leggings, though he couldn't be sure amidst the detritus.

He could not, however, bring himself to look at her face. He knew that by doing so he would lose something; something within him would surely die. Whether it was innocence, naivety, or the final, flickering embers of childish hope and optimism, he knew that looking into the dead eyes of an actual, real-life corpse would signal the definitive end of some unnamed and nebulous chapter in his life.

He turned away from his grizzly discovery, pulled his phone out of his pocket and unlocked the screen. Bringing up the call tab, he hit the number nine twice and then hesitated. He stood staring at his phone for what seemed like an eternity, before closing down his phone. Pocketing the mobile, Alan slowly turned back round and looked again at the decaying corpse laying three or four meters ahead of him. He crossed this distance with a purposeful stride, knelt beside the husk, took a handful of hair in his hand and turned the head to face his own.

"Sorry, I still feel like shit, but hopefully I'll be back in tomorrow. Sorry boss, Cheers, AJ" - SEND.

The text had been sent a little earlier today, as Alan had woken strangely alert at 6:30am, despite having caught only an hour two of broken, turbulent sleep, filled with half-realised images of decay and an overwhelming feeling of suffering.

The previous afternoon and night-time were a total blur to Alan. He had clearly untied Kratos and walked the dog home at some point, this much he knew, at which point he probably showered before feeding the dog. Did he play video games upon his return? He wasn't sure, though he did have a vague recollection of a controller in his hand. Had he watched a movie? He honestly couldn't say, so confused was his mind. There had been wine, though, that much he could say with absolute clarity. Texting in sick to work had been a no-brainer, and work was probably the furthest thing from his mind today - even further away than it usually was, even when he was actually there, sat at his desk.

Did that really happen yesterday? For real? No way, it can't have. Just me and my imagination, he thought.

Nevertheless, he had already resolved to go back and check, even before the thought had actually crystallized in his mind - base instinct over conscious decision making, it would see.

He wasted little time in drinking a strong cup of coffee, before once again donning his walking clothes and shooing a whimpering Kratos back into the hall and away from the now open front door. Alan was going back, but he was going alone. He pulled up his hood and placed his hands into his pockets as he set off. His earphones were conspicuous by their absence today, and Alan's journey was eerily quiet.

Down the road, over the field, and onto the farm tracks he went, before proceeding straight for about a kilometre and a half until he reached the turning which would lead him back on himself. From there, he would usually make his way round a small group of houses before the path naturally pointed him back toward home. He did not take this turn today, determined as he was to retrace the previous day's fateful steps toward the black hole in the shape of the dead woman. He had begun to think of this spot as a black hole since the whole world seemed to be sucked away into nothingness in this dark place; the torn fence an event horizon, to his mind. On he pressed, his legs feeling heavier with each step.

He was suddenly gripped by a thought, and a wave of fear ran through his gut. He had disturbed the integrity of the carpet, further exposing the body, so what if the newly freed aroma had attracted animals, the police, or - he smiled in spite of himself - dog walkers?

His fears were allayed upon squeezing through the narrow gap in the fence and venturing a few yards into the overgrown wilderness beyond. Having already picked and pushed his way through the green veil the day before, his passing was easier this time around. On he went and there she was, undisturbed and exactly as he had left her. He felt a relief at this, though he still didn't quite understand why. He knelt down beside her and couldn't help but wonder if he should perhaps give her a name, maybe even a back-story.

No, no I shouldn't do that; that's fucking sick, he thought.

Still, here she was. She had clearly been here a while which would perhaps suggest that nobody was looking for her, or not looking for her *here*, at least, He lived in this area and had not seen any police searches, nor had he heard anything on the local news, come to think of it. No, she must have been dumped here by someone from beyond these parts, certainly by someone far outside of Alan's bubble, at very least.

Dana. The thought came unbidden, but very firmly to his mind. Her hair was a reddish colour, like that of the character Dana Scully from the X-Files. He had loved the show and had carried a torch for the character as a teenager, so "Dana" it was. Recoiling slightly at this new-found level of familiarity, Alan nevertheless remained in place, kneeling by Dana's side.

How long he stayed there he couldn't say for sure, but there he was, hidden from the world at large, staring into the unseeing, milky eyes of this poor, discarded soul lying here in secret, stretched out before him in a ghastly approximation of the sleep which had so eluded him of late.

There he sat a while longer, staring in morbid fascination. He noted that, yes, she was dead, but she was still *here*, still occupying the same spot on the planet as himself. Her eyes were dead, her hair dishevelled. Her skin was a pallid, sickly hue, with legs long and bent to an awkward angle and small breasts leaving tell-tale traces in her vest…

He suddenly felt an all-too familiar twinge in his jogging bottoms and again recoiled in horror at a new realisation. He was becoming aroused; aroused by a *corpse*.

Still, he remained in place, the silence now deafening in his ears and every sense alert lest he be discovered in his macabre courtship. Hand trembling, he snapped a branch off a nearby tree and tentatively eased it toward the strap of Dana's vest.

Manipulating it with all the caution and precision of a surgeon, he loosened the strap and revealed a small, round breast, albeit one which had long since lost its natural colour. Far from revulsion, however, this - inexplicably - served to arouse both Alan's suspicions and his body even further. Almost outside of himself now, as if looking down on someone he recognised but did not know, Alan cautiously reached down and placed his hand inside his…

No! No, that's enough.

Snatching himself away as if it had been a burning hot pan he had touched, he threw the formerly red carpet back over Dana's body and marched away from the scene as quickly as his shaking legs would carry him.

Once he was home again and Kratos had been fed and let out into the garden to hopefully tire himself out, Alan sat and tried to make sense of earlier events. This was certainly new to him; he'd never, even in his darkest, most base moments, ever considered himself to be someone capable of becoming sexually aroused by a corpse; a grey, rotting, decaying husk wrapped in a carpet.

He rushed to the bathroom to vomit his guts up in disgust, revulsion, shame, and fear. Once he had wiped his face clean and composed himself, Alan's mind once again turned to the prospect of work in the morning. With persistent spots of vomit still entwined in his lazy whiskers, he headed back downstairs to grab a tumbler and a bottle of whiskey which a friend of his had left behind months ago following a night of drinks and video games, and which still sat untouched in the fridge.

He wanted to get out ahead of the inevitable, so he sent a message to his boss to say he intended to see out the rest of the week at home, just to be safe. He was going to be deep in the shit when he eventually returned to work, but that would have to wait, it was something he'd just have to worry about later.

The light was now fading and the evening was well and truly drawing in. Alan continued to pour and drain the whiskey with a gusto which surprised even him; then again, he'd been surprising himself a lot of late. He sat and thought. And drank. And thought. And drank until night finally pulled the curtain down on the day of all days and Kratos was snoozing blissfully on his bed. Alan was drunk enough that he felt it but not so much that he was at risk of falling and stumbling over. He was not too drunk to stand up, not too drunk to grab his hoodie and check the battery level on his phone, nor was he too drunk to unlock the door and head out into the night.

Thirty or so minutes later and in pitch darkness but for his glowing phone screen, Alan reached the yawning mouth of the opening in the fence. More than simply a portal into another world, it was now a tantalising doorway through which lay a forbidden fruit - though a rotten, mealy fruit it may be.

He reached the hallowed ground and threw back the carpet to behold Dana, her cheeks still sunken, her eyes still shark-like and lifeless, her small breast still exposed. He removed the remainder of her soiled and soaked clothing, did likewise with his own, and slid himself into her.

He awoke the next day with a blinding headache and a vague, disjointed feeling of dread. Alan sat up and drank down fully on the tumbler of whisky which he discovered at his bedside, not remembering that he had taken the bottle up to bed and fallen asleep before he'd finished it. As his eyes adjusted to the light and his ghostly thoughts coalesced into something tangible, a spectre bringing ill-tidings in the early morning glow, the horror of the previous night pressed down upon him like a ton weight, and he could hardly breathe with the dawning realisation of what he had done.

Unblinking, unmoving for several long minutes, one thought above all others flashed across his mind - *DNA*.

They would think it was him. They'd find her eventually, and they would perform a post-mortem examination and swab her for DNA, especially in her private regions given the circumstances - he'd seen enough crime dramas and documentaries to be absolutely sure of that.

What the fuck am I gonna do? What have I done?

The conflict of his past transgressions versus his potential future actions clashed in his mind like heavyweight boxers, and he rode this wave for as long as he could bear before there was only one clear course of action, futile as it may ultimately prove - but he had to do *something*.

He jumped out of bed and threw on some clothes, grabbed and leashed Kratos, and slung a bulging satchel over his shoulder before setting off into the mid-morning sunshine. He passed the old man from across the road and flashed his most earnest smile, throwing a hasty salute in the man's direction. Two middle-aged runners passed them by a few minutes later, no doubt trying to shift some of those extra pounds they were so obviously carrying, and their appearance startled Kratos into a fit of excited tail-wagging.

"Settle down! Fucking dog..." he said, more to the runners than to Kratos, and pleasantries were exchanged.

This is good, he thought. *Just out walking the dog; just one of the crowd. Nothing to see here, move along.*

They would approach the fork in the path soon, where the route turned homeward by bearing to the right, and Dana lay further ahead, on through the rough terrain. Another runner approached, a girl he recognised from around the area. She was maybe a few years younger than him, and he thought her quite pretty but not stunning.

What's her name? Caitlin? Catherine? Fuck it, something like that, he mused.

She smiled and waved pleasantly as she passed, sparing a beaming glance and an audible "*Awww,*" in Kratos' direction.

Fucking dog.

He waited until he was sure she had passed them by on her journey to who-knew where and proceeded to head on through the rough toward the hallowed ground ahead. Pushing through the fence, he tied Kratos to a tree which was not too far in, but also not too close to the path before proceeding toward Dana. Once again, he found her exactly as he had left her: naked, legs parted, a twisted analogue of a coveted centrefold. Opening his satchel, Alan pulled out the bleach and cleaning products he had brought along.

Wearing comically pink marigolds, he set about Dana's genital area, working both externally and internally, with bleach, scouring pads, disinfectant wipes; pretty much every household cleaning product he was able to fit into his satchel without arousing the suspicions of passers-by.

Once he had done all he could reasonably do to destroy the traces of his indiscretions, he replaced the goods in his bag, retrieved Kratos, and head back home as per the plan, such as it was. Alan saw out the rest of the day with too much nervous energy coursing through his veins to really accomplish anything or entertain himself in any meaningful way. Come nightfall, his sleep was a tormented blur of anguish and desperation. Tossing and turning, sweating despite the late Autumn chill, his teeth ground and scraped of their own volition. A peaceful sleep this was not.

He woke early; he was ready to commence the next phase of his hastily cobbled together plan. Once dressed, he grabbed Kratos and his phone, and set off once again in the direction of Dana, making damn sure to be seen by and to speak to as many passers-by as humanly possible despite the earliness of the hour. This he did with relative success, once again noting that the presence of Kratos acted like a magnet for the greetings and pleasantries of strangers.

Upon reaching the site a short time later, he performed one final sweep for evidence, though *what* he was actually looking for he did not know for sure. Satisfied that he had not left anything incriminating behind, he took a few deep breaths and dialled 999.

Making sure to affect a panicked, mortified voice to the best of his ability, he explained that his dog had gotten loose and, upon chasing after him through some rough ground, he had stumbled upon a dead body wrapped in a carpet. Later that evening, once the police, the ambulance crews, and the coroner had arrived to remove the body and take Alan's official statement, he was once again sat at home with a drink in his hand.

"Yes, Officer," he had said "he must have caught the scent and he just got away from me, Officer… No, we usually turn off much sooner and loop back on ourselves, but he's always been a bit of a puller, Officer."

For his part, the Officer had smiled - a dog owner himself, apparently.

"Yeah, I know the type," he had said. "Don't worry, and thanks again for calling us; it's always a dog walker that finds 'em, isn't it?" he had reassured Alan placing a fatherly hand on his shoulder.

Could he have actually pulled it off? He wondered.

They didn't take a DNA sample from me, he thought. *They fucking didn't take one! Don't celebrate just yet, though. They will, eventually. There'll be an investigation, and they'll come knocking.*

He took in and then blew out a deep, calming breath, and poured himself a glass of wine with a surprisingly steady hand. This he drank slowly, listening to some relaxing music before he attempted once again to court sleep.

"No, it's not that, mate," Alan explained to his boss.

"My stomach is fine now. It's just, with what happened the other day, you did hear didn't you? Yeah, okay. Yeah, I'm still just a bit shook up and need to get my head straight. Yeah. Uh-huh. Yeah. No, I know. Okay, will do, cheers."

He hated speaking to his boss on the phone like that, but he was no longer being allowed to merely text in sick. His boss had all but demanded to speak to him, discovery of a corpse notwithstanding. He didn't dwell on it, he had more pressing concerns.

This day, too, passed in something of a blur for Alan. He poured himself a very early glass of wine to steady his morning nerves and tried to busy himself with housework and tending to the dog. Once a few of his household jobs were done, he decided to play a few rounds on a video game before idly picking at his out-of-tune guitar for a few minutes. He could feel his frustration mounting. He found that nothing really held his attention for long - a fact that was wholly unsurprising given current circumstances.

Looking to eliminate potential obstacles and control the situation as best he could, he decided to email his boss and put in an extended period of absence, thinking two weeks should buy him enough time to wrestle some normality back into his life. He may not have a job to back to once this is over, such were the liberties he had taken of late, but he couldn't afford to think about that right now. He could only thing about Dana. The way she looked, her smell, the way she *felt*....

Stop it, Alan, he thought, trying to literally shake the thoughts out of his head with limited success. The difficult days turned to restless nights, and each day's walk with Kratos afforded him a look, albeit from a safe distance, in the approximate direction of the newly-dubbed "crime scene", complete with police tape and the obvious signs of heavy foot traffic.

Just over a week had passed since his fateful phone call to the police, and the activity on the ground had now ceased, the scene long since scoured for evidence. The press were treating the site as nothing but a random dumping spot, and the police were convinced - as was Alan - that the actual murder had indeed taken place a long way from here, and an investigation was now under way.

Of Dana herself, the noises from the press suggested that she was likely a prostitute or a drug addict, which served to explain why there had been no signs of a search or even a missing person report filed prior to Alan's call.

That night, Alan felt strangely nostalgic and inexplicably sad. He had not killed the girl himself, of course, and the guilt he felt for the acts he *had* performed was nothing compared to the *longing* he now felt knowing that the body had been removed and the site sanitised. The police, he thought, have still left him alone thus far.

Probably because she was only dumped here, she wasn't from *here,* he rationalised.

The night had once again cast its impenetrable veil over the day's proceedings and gave Alan an idea. With Kratos now sleeping soundly in the hall, he pulled his hood up over his head, stowed a bottle of wine in his satchel, he headed off to the crime scene. To do exactly *what*, he wasn't completely sure.

He picked his way through the brush, ducking and stretching in turn to negotiate the criss-crossing police tape, until he found himself once again upon the spot with which he had become so intimately familiar, though a spot now devoid of carpet, devoid of detritus, and devoid of Dana.

He sat down on the dirt and the mulch, absent-mindedly noting the plethora of impressions left on the ground by stomping police boots.

I should have been a tracker, he thought somewhere in the back of his mind.

Sitting silently for a good half hour and simply staring through the darkness into the space ahead of him, he eventually took the wine from his satchel and unscrewed the cap.

Only the best, he thought sarcastically, and chuckled in spite of himself.

He took a huge gulp from the bottle and poured a long stream onto the ground in the approximate location Dana's broken body had previously lain. He immediately regretted the pointlessly sentimental waste of good wine, and he remained in place a while longer, lost in his thoughts. When the bottle ran dry and the midnight cold had begun to gnaw at his bones, he casually discarded the empty bottle and slung his satchel back over his shoulder. Alan set off home to no doubt lay awake and stare at the ceiling before finally submitting to an hour or two of tormented sleep, visited by visions of dead, milky eyes, broken legs, and naked, deathly-pale breasts.

A few days had passed since Alan's bizarre, alcohol-fuelled midnight farewell and, for the first time in a while, he woke feeling refreshed following a semi-decent night's sleep which had thankfully lacked the tooth-grinding, the sweating, and the overall restlessness which had so badly plagued him of late.

Alan had breakfasted and showered early, and Kratos too was happily fed and watered ahead of their usual schedule. Collecting the dog's lead and the small roll of green plastic bags which he kept in a box beside the door and called Kratos for his morning expedition. Out of the village and over the field they went, toward the tracks behind the farmlands the pair knew so well.

Back to normality, he thought, or rather hoped, as they walked, determined to simply stick to their tried and tested route, putting the entire Dana incident both figuratively and literally behind them.

"Hello," he said to an old man he did not recognise as he passed close to them.

"Morning," he bade to a couple approximately his own age, who replied in kind and *awwed* at the dog. Pressing on, they inevitably approached the fork in the tracks. Inhaling deeply, Alan decided to go and give it one last look; one final peek *for old time's sake.*

He forged through the rough and pushed beyond the gap in the fence he knew so well before tying Kratos to the tree *he* knew so well. He took a moment or two to himself and began to once again feel the familiar *ache* he had genuinely tried to suppress; a mere memory to forcibly banish.

He missed it. He missed *her*.

He shook it off as best he could, recalling his resolve to move on and forget the whole torrid affair. He started back through the rough terrain toward a whimpering Kratos.

"Hello? Is anyone in there? Hello? Whose dog is this?"

The voice, female and relatively young, issued from Kratos' approximate direction, sounding at once confused and a little annoyed at the discovery of a seemingly abandoned dog. Panicking in spite of himself - he wasn't doing anything wrong, at the end of the day - he doubled his pace toward his dog and the unknown owner of the voice he had heard. As he emerged from cover and back in sight of Kratos, he recognised the girl from what now seemed like another lifetime - the runner, the pretty one who had smiled at him and the dog; *Clara* or whatever her name was.

"Hi, sorry… He's mine. Sorry if we startled you, I was just…" he began, meaning to explain how he'd just gone to, you know, gone to…

He never finished his sentence; some base, primal instinct having kicked in at that exact moment. Before he really knew what was happening, he had one hand over the girl's mouth and the other around her throat. Kicking and struggling under Alan's weight, and with Kratos' whimpering masking her muffled cries for help, the girl's eyes began to darken. Alan held her gaze, unblinking, until she kicked her last and struggled no more.

In a daze, he grabbed her by the ankles and started dragging her backwards, further back into the rough, inching inexorably closer to where his beloved Dana once rested.

With his hands held out in front of him and tears rising in his eyes, he screamed; a guttural, animalistic scream fuelled by pain, anguish and, from somewhere in the very depths of his soul, *victory*. Then, as quickly as he had surrendered it, calmness returned to him. His shaking limbs now steadied, his countenance was a mask of resigned indifference.

Slowly but with purpose, he strode silently toward Kratos, whose shoulders and hind legs were now shaking with fear. Kneeling down in front of his dog, his one companion in this world, his *best friend*, he kissed him long and deeply on the top of his soft, warm, furry little head. Then, cupping the dog's left cheek with his own right hand, he brutally and repeatedly dashed the poor creature's head against the base of the tree to which he was still tied, killing him where he stood.

His hands and arms were now covered in the viscera which had once been his dog's face, and he strode back to the runner's body, already starting to lose its colour and heat despite the sunlight attempting to break through the canopy of trees and vegetation in which they were hidden.

Despite the blood throbbing in the corners of his eyes, Alan noted that the wine bottle he had discarded here the other night was still here, its thick, green base protruding from the soggy undergrowth. He snatched it up with a hand still slick with blood and smashed it hard against the nearest tree. He regarded the newly jagged edges for a moment, then immediately stabbed, hacked, and slashed at his own wrists with the broken bottle, it too now slick with blood.

Once he had exhausted his wrists with the broken bottle, he allowed himself to fall into a strange approximation of a sitting position, his wrists ablaze with agony yet somehow numb at the same time. He could feel his life ebbing from him in a very real, tangible sense. There he sat, slumped and dying on the spot in which his life had *truly* ended weeks earlier, surrounded by the twisted body of an innocent passer-by, and a gory mound which had once been his beloved dog.

As his pulse slowed and his strength faded, his eyes began to darken and one final though flashed unbidden across his mind.

You know who'll find us, don't you, Kratos?

Fucking dog walkers.

<u>Epilogue</u>

The local news was calling it a "murder-suicide," and TV newsreaders stayed professionally detached and emotionless as they informed the masses that:

"...the bodies of two people - one male, one female - and the remains of a small dog, have been discovered in a secluded area of land adjacent to a popular dog walking route in the rural community of...."

More tantalising to the media and the masses than the discovery, however, was the location and identity of the deceased male.

"In a shocking turn of events, the bodies were found in the exact spot from which another body was removed some weeks earlier, and the deceased male is thought to be the same gentleman who actually discovered and reported the first body. The police are rumoured to

be looking into this as a potential new line of enquiry, though no official comment has yet been made on the matter..."

As with all such news items, a splash of local flavour was inevitably added to the reports, to further accentuate the horror and tragedy inflicted upon such a small rural locality. Various individuals from the area were asked to comment on the story, going in front of the camera either to express their shock and bewilderment or to suggest they always knew there was something strange about Alan.

"I always knew there was something strange about Alan..." said a sixty-five-year-old gentleman named Mr Bryce.

"You can just tell sometimes with some people, you know?"

A younger girl, perhaps twenty or twenty-one had a different opinion on the situation, saying:

"It's really sad.... I'd spoken to him a few times and he was always nice to me. I remember just this summer he stood back and let me go first in line when that battered old ice cream van came round. It's just so sad."

THE RECURRING NIGHTMARE

"Yes, Officer, that's right. Exactly like I told you five minutes ago. And five minutes before that. How many more times do I have to tell you the same fucking story?"

"Just one more time so we can be sure of what happened. Just start at the beginning. Go back to Monday night and tell us what happened from there. This is a very serious charge you're facing, Carl"

Monday, September 1st

Elizabeth and Carl Jackson had gone to bed around 10pm, as they usually did on school nights. So tired were they from long days at their respective workplaces that it was not long at all before books were put aside with barely a chapter read between them. Carl leant over and turned the light off with a grunt, and he and Elizabeth exchanged a loving *good night* before they each turned over to get some much-needed sleep.

Mondays are horrible, Carl thought to himself as he replayed the events of the day in his head. He had turned up for work tired and aching, and his inability to motivate himself made the day drag, with each hour that passed feeling more like a month as time stretched out like an elastic band.

Horrible.

Carl tried to forcibly banish these thoughts, to quieten his mind and succumb to sleep.

Sleep, as it turned out, was not long in coming and he was soon floating along blissfully on the currents of his dreams. He had always possessed a vivid imagination, and his dreams were invariably the weird and wonderful kind that are often a shame to wake from, so fanciful are their characters and so outlandish are their settings. However, as happens so often in dreams, the fantastical quests and epic adventures playing out in Carl's head soon altered their course and turned down darker, more sinister roads, and a stifling disquiet settled heavily upon Carl's sleeping mind.

In his dreams as surely as in reality, Carl was in his own bed and sleeping next to his wife. In the darkness, he could just make out the vague shape of something scuttling across the ceiling directly above him. Frozen in terror, the stillness of the night matched the stillness in Carl's very bones as he watched, helpless, while the creature ceased its horrifying skittering and began to descend slowly toward him. As the creature's silken thread extended, and the thing inched its way inexorably closer to his face in the pitch darkness, Carl tried in vain to scream.

"Babe! Babe! Wake up! Carl! Wake up!" Elizabeth was yelling as she shook her moaning and squirming husband in the dim light of her now illuminated bedside lamp. Carl's eyes sprung open at the sound of his wife's voice, but he did not immediately know what was happening. He looked to Elizabeth with fear and confusion etched onto his face, and she elaborated.

"You were having a nightmare. You were moaning and thrashing about in your sleep. Was it the spider again?"

The mere mention of the spider brought the nightmare back to Carl's mind in vivid technicolour, and he shuddered involuntarily as he remembered.

"Yeah," he said. "The spider. Again."

Elizabeth regarded him with sympathy as she reassured him - not for the first time - that it was just a dream. *There was no spider.*

Carl managed to reclaim his breathing and slow his pounding heart. Elizabeth kissed him gently on the forehead and turned the bedside lamp off in a bid to try to get at least a few more hours sleep in before the inevitable ringing of alarms beckoned them out of bed and to work once more.

Every time, Carl thought, annoyed at himself.

Every fucking time…

The dream had plagued him for years, for as long as he could remember in fact. It was the same every time. The spider would scuttle across the ceiling or the bedroom walls, only to descend toward his frozen, terrified face, and the fear he felt always prevented him from so much as moving a muscle or crying out in response. He had always woken up - or *been* woken up - before the creature actually made footfall on his skin.

He genuinely feared what would happen if that ever changed.

Tuesday, September 2nd

Another day at work soon presented itself, and with it another dose of stress and anger. This time it was Elizabeth's turn to bemoan the cretins she was surrounded by on a daily basis upon her return home. They ate a light meal and retired to bed early, where Elizabeth vented her frustrations to Carl. They put the world to rights for a good fifteen minutes and felt better once their respective bosses and colleagues had been either killed in the most outlandish ways possible or, at very least, told to go fuck themselves. Well, in their minds, at least.

Sleep once again came quickly to Carl and he was snoring within minutes. Under the soothing blanket of slumber which the darkness had pulled over him, he chuckled out loud at a joke he had told himself in his dreams, and lay smiling at whatever it was which held so jovial a grip on his thoughts. The peace, however, did not last, and the smile on Carl's face quickly contorted itself into a grimace. His formerly smooth forehead had become creased and his teeth ground audibly with the stress placed on his body by his subconscious.

It was back.

It came from further away this time, emerging from the loft-hatch on the landing just outside their bedroom before crossing the threshold into his and Elizabeth's private space. The space that should have been safe, the one place to which no intruder, demon, nor spectre should be granted access. The bedroom should have been

Carl's safe-haven - his sanctuary - but that's not how nightmares work.

  Onward it crawled, crossing the distance between door and bed in short order - or maybe it was forever, such is the nature of time in dreams - and it was upon him. It sat perched on the ceiling above Carl's paralysed head, as if waiting for some unseen signal to begin its dark descent. It soon received whatever signal it had been waiting for, some black flag waved somewhere beyond Carl's sphere of vision and influence. The spider spread its thick legs and began to lower itself on silken thread. On and on it came, and dream-Carl could not so much as blink as his lifelong tormentor came to call once more.

 This time he did not need Elizabeth to wake him, as they were both ripped from their respective sleep by the sudden and unmistakable sound of breaking - no, *smashing* - glass, as a flailing Carl sent his bedside glass of water careening into the bedroom wall.

 "What the fuck?" shouted Elizabeth, jumping up and turning on the bedside light simultaneously. Her eyes darted left and right as she quickly assessed the situation, then closed her eyes and let out a deep sigh as the realisation dawned on her.

  "Again?" she asked, with an almost imperceptible but very much existent edge of frustration her voice.

  "I… it…the…" Carl attempted to explain, pointing out the glass, the ceiling, and then the bed one after another.

"Go clean up and bandage your hand, I'll sort this mess out," said Elizabeth, and it was only then that Carl noticed the blood running down his hand and wrist.

"So that's how you hurt your hand, then? Knocked over a glass?" the officer asked.

"Yes, exactly like I've already told you five fucking times." Carl *snapped, the bare walls in the small interview room starting to close in on him as they echoed his pained voice around and around.*

"Watch your language. Okay, go on; what happened next?"

Wednesday, September 3rd

Carl's mood that day was dark, and his temper was short. The pain in his hand was nothing compared to the anger in his very bones. Toward whom his anger was directed, he knew all too well, and that was the problem.

Myself, he mused.

It irked him greatly that a nightmare he had endured since childhood was still plaguing him in his thirties and had not only robbed him of restful sleep but had now caused him physical injury.

He tried to exhale his anger upon returning home, and whilst the sight of his wife had indeed alleviated some of his stress, he still felt it in his stomach and granted himself an early night. He read for half an hour without really taking in any of the story, absent-mindedly checked his social media for ten minutes, and turned the light off in the hope of courting a restful, dreamless sleep.

He dozed for a while before eventually succumbing to a sleep so deep, he neither heard nor felt Elizabeth come to bed a few hours later. His dreams began the way they usually did, full of surreal imagery and fantastical scenarios, even the odd joke or two to make his sleeping face smile in spite of itself.

But this peace did not last, it never did. Soon his bright, colourful dreams took on a paler, more muted hue, until his mind was shrouded in darkness. His dream-senses were dulled as the darkness swallowed his perception, and then he saw it.

It was much larger this time, and he could make out each leg, eye, and pincer without issue even in the pitch darkness of his mind. It took up a position on the ceiling directly above his head and began its nightly incursion downward, suspended by its unnaturally thin thread.

Carl's heart was gripped by icy cold fingers as his fear and panic threatened to overwhelm him. He did not know if he would be able to survive actual contact with the nightmare creature which was slowly descending toward his face.

Elizabeth's cry woke him from his hell, and as he wiped his sweat-soaked brow with the back of his hand he beheld his wife in the light of her bedside lamp, and a wave of disgust and shame ran through him at the sight.

She was crying and holding her face.

"For fuck sake Carl! You fucking punched me!" she yelled at him. Her nose was bleeding and she recoiled from his outstretched hands.

"Babe I… I'm so sorry. It was the…." he began.

"The spider, I know, Carl! It's getting fucking ridiculous! You need to speak to someone or take a pill or something! This can't go on."

Elizabeth snatched up her pillows and left the room, leaving Carl laying there all alone, soaked in sweat and drowning in guilt. She went to the bathroom to clean up her nose before retiring to the guest bedroom in an attempt to get some sleep. Carl lay awake for hours, and whether sleep eluded him of its own volition or whether his subconscious did not want it to come and was actively trying to stave it off, he couldn't quite decide.

Thursday, September 4th

Not again, Carl thought.

I'm not having another night like that. I'm just so fucking tired.

He was quiet at work, owing in part to his tiredness and in equal part to his shame. Elizabeth had left for work early that morning without muttering so much as a word to him. At around lunch time Carl knocked on his boss' door and asked to take Friday off work; despite the comically short notice, his boss allowed it. Carl left work and travelled home via the local shop and was home before he knew it. Putting both of the recently purchased bottles of wine in the fridge, he set about making an evening meal for when Elizabeth came home.

A little later Elizabeth was back and, luckily for Carl, was actually speaking to him again. She knew the dreams were not his fault, that they must be a manifestation of some traumatic event in his childhood, and the look on his face as she walked through the door amused her, though she knew it shouldn't. They ate a terrific meal and opened one of the bottles.

Now that all was once again well with the couple, Carl wanted to give his wife a nice, peaceful night's sleep. If that also meant a dreamless slumber for him at the price of a blinding headache and cotton mouth the following morning, so be it.

Later that evening, once Elizabeth had gone to bed - *she,* at least, still had to work in the morning - Carl poured himself a full glass of wine and settled comfortably on the sofa to play a few video games to pass the time. The first glass having barely touched the sides, Carl paused the game and treated himself to a refill.

A few hours later, both bottles were empty, and Carl felt a tiredness the likes of which he had not felt in a long, long time. His footwork was sorely lacking in grace, but he meandered his way upstairs regardless, not even bothering to stop and brush his teeth.

He collapsed into bed, and the next thing he knew, he was peeking through dry, scratchy eyes, as Elizabeth kissed him on the forehead and announced her exit for work. He immediately fell back to sleep.

"Okay, well, we have the empty bottles in evidence, and your blood test showed a significant amount of alcohol still in your system, so that part at least makes sense," the officer said to Carl.

"So now we come to Friday, and this is the part I need you to go over again, in as much detail as you can remember."

Friday, September 5th

Carl's Friday was a torrid affair as his hangover prevented him from really doing anything, or at least doing anything effectively. Once he had finally decided that he had to get up before he missed the entire day, he proceeded to merely slouch his way around the house, never far from the sofa, and never far from a glass of water. He stared at the TV whilst the newsreaders retold the same four or five stories, and eventually decided to just veg out in front of a superhero DVD he'd already seen a hundred times.

Elizabeth had no sympathy for him upon her return home from work but was secretly a little concerned by the lengths to which her husband had gone to avoid dreaming. To avoid *that* dream.

When night came, Carl was extremely eager to crawl back into bed given the way he had been feeling all day. Still, his mind was clear, and he had at least slept soundly the night before.

Optimistic that he might have trained - or drank - his mind out of the dreams, or at least banished them for a while, Carl said goodnight to Elizabeth, closed his eyes, and turned over.

It did not take long for his dreams to turn dark, despite the wave of nausea he was still riding. Images of walls, ceilings, bathroom sinks, loft hatches, towels, creases in curtains - all of the mundane, everyday items he had come to associate with the mortal dread of hidden creatures, flashed through his mind.

And then it emerged.

As if to make up for its absence the previous night, it was colossal in stature as it stared at him from its lofty perch. Though it was upside down on the ceiling, Carl could still make out the clacking of its mandibles which made it look as if it were addressing him in some ghastly, alien tongue. He could almost hear the creature speaking directly into his mind, taunting him, and ice-cold fear washed over him as if it had been thrown from a bucket. His heart was racing.

"Did you miss me? I missed you," the giant spider said, its grotesque mandibles unmoving as if it were somehow willing the words directly into Carl's panicked mind.

"You can't escape… I've always been here; I will *always be here."*

It began its descent.

Whether it was the memory of Elizabeth's bloodied nose, or his own despair at being so beholden to this nightmare, something snapped inside of Carl. He felt some semblance of control returning to his limbs, and he found that he could move his fingers despite the terror stabbing at him like liquid nitrogen in his veins. His fingers first, then his arms. Dream-Carl could now move.

He reached out just in time to grab the creature before it landed fully on his face.

"I've got you… I've got you now you fucker."

He adjusted his body so that the creature was no longer above his head but beneath him. It was pinned firmly to the bed and unable to escape as he squeezed.

"Leave me the fuck alone! I hate you!" dream-Carl screamed with everything he had, every ounce of hatred in his body pouring into his muscles.

He squeezed the enormous, squirming creature with all the strength he could muster, and felt a satisfying *pop* as his thumbs found its eyes.

As he pushed and pushed, harder and harder he drove his thumbs into the creature's eye sockets. With his teeth bared and his skin taut against his veins, he felt warm blood oozing over his hands and wrists.

Still he pushed and still he squeezed, vaguely aware of Elizabeth screaming from somewhere outside of himself, and vaguely aware that the spider only had two eyes.

THE MIDNIGHT MAN

Crime was rampant in the northern city of Midbrook; it always had been. A region once prosperous with steelworks and ship building had long since been left behind, abandoned by the political elite, and left to rot in the shadow of automation and globalisation.

The money was gone and the spotlight with it. Where there were once riches, drugs now ruled. Where things were once created, abandoned buildings, and graffitied ruins now stood as testament to the social decay which had set in long ago.

The old Odeon cinema was once considered the number one hangout for families and shy teenage lovers. For decades, children had gazed in awe at spaceships and aliens, as nervous boys put trembling arms around their blushing dates. But those days were long gone, and the cinema was now a boarded-up husk.

In the alley behind the old cinema, half-hidden in darkness at this late hour, the pleading cries of a young man rang out loud, but nobody came.

Nobody ever came.

"Please! Let me go! I just want to go home… I got lost, that's all, I'll turn round and go straight home!" he pleaded through tears, snot, and blood.

"Hahaha! I don't think so," said the bigger man, shoving the boy hard toward two more thugs.

"Yeah, finders-keepers, and we found *you,"* grinned the second, extending the blade of his knife with a metallic *flick.*

"Please! No! Please don't kill me! Please, I…" cried the boy, while the three men laughed as they shoved him around between them, clearly reveling in his fear.

The knife-wielding man never knew what hit him. One second he was casually juggling the blade from one hand to the other, advancing on the boy, and the next his head was smashed into the alley wall by a gloved hand, shattering his teeth and rendering him unconscious in an instant.

His companions - just as surprised as their leader - stared in confusion and amazement, but only for a moment before regaining what little wits they had about them.

"What the fuck?! Who *is* that?! Get him!"

He was a blur of motion, a shadow moving among them. The jolting crack of an armoured fist connecting with a chin preceded the sickening crunch of an arm snapping the wrong way at the elbow. Within mere moments the three assailants were face-down on the wet, dirty concrete, either unconscious or mewling in pain.

The dark figure grabbed each in turn by the ankle and dragged them out from the darkness of the alleyway and onto the deserted main street, where he planted one devastating right fist into each assailant's face to ensure they were indeed out cold. Satisfied that the thugs were no longer a threat to the young man in the alley, the mystery man removed a can of spray paint from the depths of his dark purple cape and sprayed a crude crescent moon shape in bright yellow on each of the thugs' chests.

A calling card, the boy thought.

The wraith turned to make his exit as stealthily as he had approached but halted as the young man discovered his voice once more.

"Wait!" he shouted; his hand outstretched toward his rescuer.

The man stopped and turned, and the boy got his first good look at him in the moonlight.

He appeared to be wearing black combat fatigues overlaid with some sort of makeshift armour, a thick purple cape pulled tightly around his shoulders, and a heavy-duty balaclava pulled down tight over his face. The man nodded almost imperceptibly, though his eyes remained hidden behind the dark goggles he wore over the balaclava, and he left.

"Whoa…" the boy whispered to himself in the darkness.

"DCI Tennant, over here!"

"Fuck, who invited the fucking press?" asked Tennant, more to himself than anybody in particular. His face changed colour as it was lit at intervals by flashing red and blue lights, despite the glare of the early morning sun.

"DCI Tennant, what can you tell us about last night's attack? Do we have a vigilante in Midbrook?" asked the reporter, a squirrelly-looking chap who reeked of cheap aftershave and was clearly still wet behind the ears.

"No comment. Now piss off and let us do our jobs," replied the DCI with not a hint of warmth in his tone nor bearing. He ducked under the crime scene tape and made his way down the alley, despite the three thugs already being in custody following their discovery by a patrol car on a random sweep in the small hours.

DCI Tennant spoke to the CSIs on the ground and looked at the tell-tale signs of the fight; clearly something big had happened.

But what, exactly? he mused.

After a few moments spent chewing his lip and tightly furrowing his brow in concentration, Tennant extricated himself from the scene and back toward his car, where he was set upon once more by the plucky young reporter.

"DCI, what more can you tell us about this vigilante? Is it true he marked his victims with a moon symbol?"

Where the fuck is he getting this from? thought Tennant. If they had a leak in their ranks, he would see to it personally that they would be fucked every which-way from here by nightfall.

"NO. COMMENT." he said in reply, emphasising each word more than was really necessary.

"But the witness we spoke to said that he saw the man use a can of spray paint to…"

"Witness? *What* witness?" interjected Tennant angrily, grabbing the young reporter by the lapels.

Now he had the DCIs attention.

"Well…. we…"

"Son, you listen to me and you listen good. Give me the name, or I will personally insert that tape recorder so far up your ass you'll be shitting cassettes before the day is out. Do I make myself clear?"

Two minutes later, Tennant had his lead.

Despite the sun sitting high in the blue, cloudless sky, all was dark and gloomy inside warehouse 52. Here on the docks, the site of Midbrook's once prosperous industrial sector, all was now in a perpetual state of decay and disrepair.

The perfect location for a secret lair.

Standing on a raised dais which once housed heavy machinery and now lay barren but for eroded metal and assorted detritus, was a tall, powerful looking man dressed in an immaculately tailored suit. His shoes were so highly polished that the hundred or so assorted thugs and goons in attendance could almost see themselves reflected in his obviously expensive footwear. The handkerchief in his left breast pocket was expertly folded and perfectly complimented his tie. Here was a man who would not look out of place in the exclusive establishments of New York or Monaco.

Except for the latex pig mask he wore to hide his face.

"The Midnight Man…" The Pig said in a booming, authoritative voice.

"The fucking *Midnight Man.*"

He held a copy of the Midbrook Gazette aloft in his right hand, and he commanded the absolute and unwavering attention of all and sundry in attendance.

"This cock-sucker puts three of our guys in the hospital, and they're calling him a hero." He turned his head slowly, taking in as many gazes as he could with piercing blue eyes that shone brightly from within the shadows of the pig mask.

"We haven't been bold enough. We need to send a bigger, louder message. You all have your assignments; do not fuck this up. Any mistakes, anyone talks, anything goes wrong at all, I will kill your children first while you watch, and you afterwards, once I've had a little fun. Now go."

As the mob of goons slowly and silently made their way out of the old warehouse and back onto the streets to begin their assigned tasks, The Pig looked down at the map which lay at his feet on the dais, the map of Midbrook, and he grinned as he stared at the nursing home he'd crudely circled in red.

Time to send the message.

Tennant's lead didn't amount to much, the kid more or less confirmed what the evidence already appeared to suggest. The police believed that an attempted mugging and assault had been interrupted by an as-yet-unidentified male in a costume. A male in a costume who had single-handedly put three criminals in the hospital. The DCI did get a better description of the man's clothing at least, and satisfied himself that there was little more the kid could give him, if anything.

"The Midnight Man. Jesus," he said under his breath as he climbed back into his car. As he was driving back to the station to complete the necessary reports and file the requisite paperwork, Tennant's mind began to wander. His train of thought took him from the kid to the vigilante, from the vigilante to his neighbourhood, and from his neighbourhood to his home. He was tired these days, always tired. Tired to his very bones. He was tired now, and his eyes started to feel heavy.

"All units, all units!" came the hail over the radio, snapping Tennant back into the here and now.

"DCI Tennant here. Go ahead dispatch, over."

"We have a major fire at the Sacred Heart Care Home. All available units to respond, over".

The words *care home* felt like a punch in the gut, and Tennant found himself praying that everyone was safe.

"Roger that, dispatch. Show me going, over."

Tennant was on the scene in less than ten minutes and, though he had been here before, he no longer recognised the place. Where once had stood a pretty, modern building, decorated brightly with a lush garden out front, now stood a blackened husk with smoke billowing and fires still burning in places. Where the garden once housed a myriad of vividly coloured flowers, black body bags now lay in their place, a sick inversion of its former beauty.

"What the fuck... Sergeant! Over here!"

The young sergeant hurried over to the DCI as commanded.

"What in God's name happened here?" demanded Tennant.

"We don't know for sure yet, Sir, but it looks deliberate. It looks like it could have been a bomb."

The younger man swallowed hard.

"A bomb? Bullshit."

"Sir, the windows and doors were blown outwards, the roof upwards, and the fire guys have found what looks to be a blast crater round the back".

Tennant did not respond immediately but merely stood in place. He tried in vain to steady his breathing as the muscles in his jaw worked against one another in a battle which played out upon his grim countenance.

"God dammit. Who would bomb a fucking OAP home? Seal it off. And nobody talks to the press!"

It was bad. Twenty-seven dead and scores injured. The site itself was totaled, and the whole city was reeling with grief and dismay. Red and blue lights lit the sky like a firework display nobody wanted, and stoic emergency workers went about their macabre tasks with brows furrowed in grim determination. Tennant's hands, face, and clothes were black with soot and reeked of smoke, and he was now back at his desk with his head in his hands.

Beep.

He looked up at his computer to see one new email sitting unread in his inbox and was just about to ignore it and head for home when he registered the text in the subject line. An involuntary chill shot down his spine.

'*Out With The Old*', it read in bold font. Tennant sat up straight in his chair and immediately clicked on the email. It contained only a link to an online video. Tennant started to think it may just be spam or a sick joke and actively considered deleting the email, but morbid curiosity took over and he clicked the link.

The video began with a few seconds of darkness and muffled crackling noises, but then panned round to reveal a tall man in a finely tailored suit.

And a latex pig mask.

"Out with the old, in with the new," the masked man began, laughing as he spoke.

"Citizens of Midbrook. By now you will have heard about the *tragedy* which occurred earlier today at the Sacred Heart Care Home. For those who have not, allow me to fill you in on the finer details. At approximately 11:30am, a group of men were sent - on my instructions - to place a bomb in the kitchen of the old folks' home. This bomb was then detonated remotely, resulting in the deaths of twenty-seven people. We had hoped for more, but beggars cannot be choosers, it would seem."

The hairs on the back of Tennant's neck were stood rigid, and a bead of sweat had begun to cascade down his forehead. He unknowingly held his breath as the video continued.

"That's right. I did this. My name is The Pig, and I'm going to blow your fucking houses down."

The video ended abruptly, and Tennant registered that it had already been viewed over thirty thousand times in the last half-hour alone.

"Shit," he muttered, finally letting out the breath he had been holding.

Within the hour it was all hands-on deck, with off-duty officers coming back into work despite the darkness which now blanketed the town. Orders were barked here and there, doors were slammed, and phones rang off the hook, with the single focus amidst the chaos being to discover anything and everything possible about this 'Pig' character. Each and every frame and pixel of the video were scrutinised and analysed in forensic detail for clues, and audio experts played back the clicks and crackles at the video's start for anything which might give away the shooting location.

So far, all efforts in this direction had been in vain.

Tennant's phone vibrated in his pocket.

'Odeon Alley. Come alone. MM' read the text.

MM? he wondered, until the penny dropped, and he sighed heavily and wearily, his temples throbbing.

The fucking Midnight Man.

He was right, of course. About half an hour after he'd made his excuses and left the precinct, Tennant was stood alone in the dark, dank alley behind the old Odeon cinema. The crime scene team had already wrapped up their investigations and had since moved on to the Sacred Heart bomb site.

Once again, Tennant's cynical mind whispered to him that this was just a prank, that nobody was coming to meet him, when he heard a low, deep voice behind him.

"DCI Tennant."

Turning to face the source of the voice in the darkness, the DCI could scarcely believe what he was seeing. It was exactly as the witness had described. Here stood a man in black combat fatigues with what looked like paintball armour over the top, a heavy balaclava and goggles, and a cape - a deep purple fucking *cape*.

"Give me one reason why I shouldn't arrest you right now and drag your Halloween-ass straight to the station," he demanded, not intimidated in the slightest by this fucker with his grandma's curtains wrapped round his shoulders.

"I'm here to help, I'm on your side," said the masked man.

"Oh yeah? And what makes you think we need your help?"

"I can go where you can't, I can do what you won't. I just need you to keep your guys off my back while I work."

There was something about the way he said that last word which intrigued Tennant, and he found himself curious despite every instinct in his body telling him to knock this guy to the kerb.

"And what would you do, exactly, were I to look the other way?" asked the DCI.

"I'll get you The Pig."

Violence: to him it was an art form. Every punch a masterful brushstroke, every kick an operatic overture. His movements were almost balletic as he moved through thug after thug, breaking arms and shattering teeth, destroying kneecaps and quite literally cracking skulls. The Midnight Man wanted answers, and this gang of low-level, street scum fuckers were going to give him them.

One by one they fell, either crying out in agony or hitting the deck hard and silently, having been rendered unconscious by this masked whirlwind. Only one remained and was now backed into a corner with the armoured vigilante approaching slowly but with clarity of purpose. The man adjusted his grip on the crowbar he so desperately clung to and started swinging wildly as he screamed.

The Midnight Man merely ducked the wayward swipes, grabbed the back of the thug's arm using his own momentum against him, and brought the limb down onto his own knee, snapping it in one fluid motion.

The thug found himself screaming once more, though now for an entirely different reason. He collapsed to the ground clutching his fractured limb, and the vigilante was on him in a second.

"Where is The Pig?" he growled.

"I… I don't know, I swear! I've never met him!" the man managed through his agonised grimace.

"You're lying!" replied the masked man, planting a gloved fist square on the thug's jaw.

"Tell me where he is!" he demanded, grabbing the thug by his jacket, and drawing him in close to his goggled eyes.

"I… I don't… he'll kill me!" pleaded the stricken goon.

The Midnight Man grabbed the thug and hauled him up onto his feet, then slammed him hard against the wall. He clutched the goon by the throat and leaned in so close he could smell the man's breath through his balaclava.

"And what makes you think I won't?" he snarled, applying pressure to the man's windpipe.

"D… D… Docks…" spluttered the thug as best as he could manage. "Tha… that's all I know…"

The vigilante head-butted the man into an unconscious oblivion and made quick work of spray-painting his symbol on the assorted goons at his feet.

So, the docks.

The Midnight Man at least knew where to start looking. The docks were an enormous area to cover, but it was a start.

An hour later, following a single brief message, the Midnight Man and DCI Tennant were standing in the darkness of the Odeon's alley once more, this having become their de facto meeting place.

"This had better be good… *Midnight Man*," said Tennant, putting a touch of mocking emphasis on his new friend's moniker.

"He's at the docks. I don't know where exactly, but it's a lead," replied the vigilante, choosing not to rise to the bait.

"Oh yeah? And how do you know that?" asked the detective, not even trying to hide his skepticism.

"His goons. They *volunteered* the information." The vigilante was now the one over-emphasising particular words.

"*Volunteered*, huh?" asked Tennant. "Like they *volunteered* themselves into the hospital earlier?"

"They…"

"You know what? I don't wanna know," said Tennant, cutting the vigilante off before he could deftly avoid answering another perfectly straightforward fucking question.

"So, what's the move, detective?"

Tennant stood perfectly still for a moment, as if lost in thought, then took a long, deep sigh.

"The way I see it, we …"

His sentence hung unfinished in the air between them as the ground shook and a huge fireball erupted in the sky about a mile south of their location.

"My god…" said Tennant, staring in disbelief at the explosion. He turned back around and found himself staring at an empty space where the Midnight Man had stood mere seconds earlier.

It was much worse this time. Sixty-seven dead, all students who had either been inside their on-campus accommodation or out drinking in the university bar. Countless others had been injured by the blast, and the blaring of sirens and the red-blue-red-blue flashing of emergency vehicle lights was blinding, even through his goggles.

The Midnight Man stood on the roof of a building not far from the university campus, surveying the scene, and could see DCI Tennant on the ground. As expected, the DCI was busy barking orders at his men and forcibly pushing away the media with their cameras, mics, and mobile phones all lit up and being waved around in the faces of the first responders.

It was carnage. A warzone brought to a university campus, one of the few remaining beacons of hope in the god-forsaken city.

Tennant was as busy and as angry as he had ever been in his *life*, let alone his career. Pulling the strings, coordinating the police response, and trying to gather a picture of exactly what the fuck had happened. He looked for all the world like a football coach shouting and gesticulating to his team from the sidelines.

Hours later, once all that could be done had been done, Tennant found himself back in his office and honestly thought that he'd probably just end up sleeping there for the night. He poured himself a stiff whiskey from his desk stash and drank it down in one gulp. Not satisfied, he poured another but hesitated just before putting it to his lips. There was a package on his desk, wrapped in brown paper and addressed to him personally. Whilst a package on his desk wouldn't usually arouse any suspicion, this one sent a shiver down his spine. There, on the side of the package, was a sticker.

A sticker bearing the image of a cartoon pig.

He opened it carefully, painstakingly, in case it was an explosive device of some kind. Instead what he beheld was an old VHS tape.

Who still uses VHS tapes? he wondered.

He put down his glass and grabbed the package. He practically ran through the precinct toward the media lounge, and once he had arrived, he immediately located the old VHS player they kept around for reviewing CCTV evidence.

He played the tape.

"DCI Tennant," began the man on the tape, his words clear despite the latex pig mask he wore. "Explosive night on campus, wouldn't you agree? My plan worked perfectly, once again. You're probably wondering '*why the video tape?*'"

He paused as if allowing the detective time to respond.

"No? Well, call me a traditionalist, but viral videos on the internet are just so... *uncivilised.* I prefer a more direct approach, so I'm reaching out to you, personally, man to man - or should that be Pig to Pig?" he chuckled to himself under the mask. "You see, right about now you'll be expecting me to make my demands, to tell you what I want so that I'll stop the killing. But the truth is, I don't really *want* anything. Do I have a problem with students or the elderly? Of course not. Do I despise the *system* and want to start a city-wide revolution? No, I don't care about any of that."

He paused, as if lost in a thought.

"This is just who I am, and who I'll continue to be. You'll never catch me; you'll never even see me coming."

The Pig reached forward toward the camera, and the recording ended abruptly.

Tennant sat in silence for what seemed like an hour but was really only a few minutes. He ejected the tape, went back to his office, and poured himself another whiskey. What he did next surprised even Tennant himself. He picked up his phone and sent a message to the Midnight Man.

My office. Now.

The vigilante arrived quickly, and Tennant showed him the tape with little preamble. Once it was over, the Midnight Man merely turned his head to look at Tennant, as if waiting for the detective to speak first.

He did.

"Well? Aren't you going to say anything?" he asked, exasperated.

"What would you like me to say? We need to stop him. That hasn't changed."

"Okay, so what the fuck are we waiting for?" replied Tennant, grabbing his coat. "You said he's at the docks? Well let's go take a look".

"No, I'll go. You go home," said the vigilante, holding up his hand in protest.

"The hell you will," said Tennant.

"It's late, detective. Go home to your family. Sleep off the whiskey. I've got this," he said, already turning and walking away. Tennant let him go and called a cab to take him home.

Midbrook had been quiet for a couple of days following the delivery of the tape and the late-night meeting in Tennant's office. The Midnight Man had scoured the docks systematically, unit by unit, but had so far found no trace of The Pig or his bumbling henchmen. He'd kept DCI Tennant updated as he went and reassured him that there was still a lot of ground to cover. Something would turn up.
Onto the next unit he went, another large, derelict warehouse. He pried open the doors and eased himself inside, moving silently in the darkness. He made his way along narrow corridors and through dark anterooms, proceeding further into the facility, then stopped dead in his tracks when he heard voices up ahead.

"This is the last one, right?"

"Yeah, I think so. I fucking hope so."

Like a shadow, he followed the voices to their source and the look of surprise and panic on the faces of the goons afforded him a grin beneath his balaclava. They dropped the large wooden crate they had been carrying between them and turned toward the vigilante, but they were too slow by a distance. Before they could register what was happening, one of them was already unconscious on the ground, his jaw shattered, and the other was in a heap clutching a broken leg in agony.

The Midnight Man flipped open the crate to check the contents inside: *dynamite*. He let out a low growl then turned and grabbed the brutalised yet still conscious goon by the hair. He picked him up and held the man's grimacing face a mere inch from his own.

"What's he planning? Where's the rest?" he screamed at the thug.

"Fuck you!" the injured man spat back in defiance.

The Midnight Man seized the man's remaining good leg and gave it an almighty twist. He heard the kneecap pop under pressure and the man screamed anew.

The vigilante pressed on.

"Tell me what he's planning! Where were you taking the explosives?"

The man didn't reply with words this time but just shook his head stoically as he clutched at his decimated legs. The Midnight Man, however, was not fucking around.

He let the thug drop back to the floor and strode purposefully over to the unconscious goon. He knelt beside him and put his arms around the man's head and neck from behind.

"Last chance, cunt! Tell me what you're up to or this fucker dies!"

The man shook his head.

"You… you wouldn't."

In one fluid motion, the Midnight Man snapped the neck of the helpless goon and released his body to the floor with a sickening thud. He held the other man's wide-eyed stare for a moment before marching back over to the surviving henchman. He flexed his significant muscle beneath his armour and grabbed the terrified thug by the throat.

"I'm asking you for the last time. Where is the Pig, and what are the explosives for?"

"Okay, okay, I'll talk. I don't know where he is. Look around you, man, he's gone, moved out! We were just picking up the last of the weapons for the… um, the…."

"THE WHAT?" demanded the vigilante, his body shaking with rage.

"The kids, man. The explosives are for the fucking kids."

The Midnight Man's fists were a blur of motion as he pounded and pounded on the other man's broken legs until he screamed like a frightened animal at slaughter.

"*Which* kids?" the masked man demanded. There must be hundreds of schools, nurseries, orphanages, and maternity hospitals in a city this size.

"I don't know, I swear! Only the guys who actually set them off know the location, man! Please, enough! That's all I know!" he protested.

"I believe you," said the Midnight Man, slowly, calmly. "So you're of no more use to me."

The Midnight Man's punches soon took on a wet, sloppy sound, and the thug's protests and screams fell silent.

The cavalry wasn't long in arriving following the vigilante's short message to Tennant. Forensic teams were combing the warehouse centimetre by centimetre, and the covered bodies of the two thugs were being loaded into the waiting coroner's vehicle.

Tennant stood in the centre of the chaos, embodying the calm in the eye of the storm, but his stillness belied the maelstrom swirling inside him. He had two dead bodies and nothing here but one crate of explosives and a layer of dust covering every surface. They were too late; The Pig had known they were closing in and had shut up shop.

He was gone and nobody knew where the fuck he was.

There was no sign of the vigilante either, and no spray-painted moon symbols had been left this time, though the DCI was in absolutely no doubt as to who had killed the thugs.

That fucker has some serious explaining to do. When I get my hands on that cape-wearing bastard.

Right on cue, his phone vibrated in his pocket.

The roof.

Tennant immediately excused himself and made his way to the maintenance stairway, taking great pains not to be seen. He soon made it to the roof and saw, standing half-hidden by the steam blown out by the automated ventilation system, the vigilante. His gloved hands, forearms, and even the dark lenses of his goggles were stained crimson with gore and viscera.

"Do you wanna tell me just what in the name of *holy fuck* happened in there?" demanded the detective.

"It's kids, Jack - he's going after kids."

"What? How do you - never mind" Tennant corrected himself, remembering the bodies and barely registering the vigilante's use of his first name. "What kids? Where?"

"They didn't know, but there must have been dozens of crates of explosives in there at one point. It's bad, detective."

"It's bad? Are you fucking kidding me? You just murdered two people and now you tell me some crazy fucker in a pig mask is planning on blowing up kids? You bet your fucked-up ass it's bad!"

"I'll find him. I'll stop him, I swear."

"Oh yeah, and how are you going to do that, huh?" replied the detective, one hand resting casually on his revolver.

"I'll tear down this whole city if I have to. I'll put every shoplifter, crack dealer, purse snatcher, and child molester in the hospital or in the ground before I let this happen," he paused, staring at the detective for a long moment, noting the hand resting instinctively on the firearm.

"I'll find him. I'll stop him. You just have to let me walk out of here."

The detective swallowed hard, squeezing the grip of the revolver, then sighed out loud as he relaxed.

"Don't make me regret this," he said, firmly. "The next time we meet, if you don't have The Pig tied up and beaten shitless, I'm bringing you in myself."

"Thank you, detective," said the vigilante as he turned and disappeared into the night.

"Go get him, Midnight Man."

Home at last.

Brian Blake - The Midnight Man - made hard work of removing his blood-soaked gloves. The pain in his fingers from the beatings he had doled out in the warehouse elicited more than a wince as he worked. Once his gloves had been removed, he proceeded to unfasten his goggles and remove his balaclava.

He moved to the bathroom to check in the mirror for the loss of teeth or for any blackening around his shockingly blue eyes. Once he was satisfied that he had come out of that last brutal encounter relatively unscathed, he continued to remove his crimson-stained clothes.

He now removed his armour and his boots. Brian decided against a shower since he was on the clock with no time to spare, and instead proceeded to the kitchen in just his boxer shorts, the bruising to his muscular body already starting to show despite the armour he wore. He poured himself a very tall, very neat whiskey which he downed in one gulp.

That hit the spot.

His throat was burning, and his belly was warm, and Brian shook off the fatigue and steeled himself for his next mission.

Back upstairs he went, picking up his discarded Midnight Man gear and stowing it away in its dust bag before hanging it lovingly in his wardrobe. From the same wardrobe he took his best, most expensive grey suit, a brand-new red tie with matching pocket handkerchief, and a highly polished pair of expensive-looking brown brogues.

He nodded to himself at his choice of outfit, then reached up to the top shelf to retrieve the latex pig mask which would complete the ensemble. He meticulously checked and double checked the stock of matches in his top dresser drawer, checked again the map which showed St Patrick's Orphanage circled in red, and began to dress.

Idiots, he thought, breaking into a wide grin.

You'll never see me coming.

Burn, baby, burn.

THE CHAIR

Greensleeves.

The metallic *clang, clang, clicketty-clang* issued from the ancient van's rooftop speakers, breaking the silence of the early hours out here in the middle of nowhere, and startling Jacob into a panic.

"Turn that shit off! Right now, Sabina!" he hissed through clenched teeth. He would have screamed were it not for the inherently covert nature of their operation.

Of roughly average height, sickly pale skinned, and perpetually tired-looking, Jacob Dancy was the owner of the vehicle and the ringleader of this merry little band. Well on his way to fifty, he had grown soft around the middle, and the thickness of his glasses had increased exponentially with each passing year.

"I'm sorry; I hit the button by accident" said Sabina, immediately cutting off the blaring din at its source.

Sabina was in her mid-thirties, and this was the first time Jacob had taken her along with him on one of his… *field trips*. He pushed his glasses up his nose and spared a glance at Bill and Dante in the back before blowing out his anger.

"I mean, who chose the music, huh? What kind of tune is Greensleeves for a fucking ice cream van?"

Around fifteen minutes later the van pulled up outside of a dilapidated, long-abandoned factory unit whose roof had begun to crumble and whose doors had long-since been broken by squatters and vagrants. It was empty now, and it would serve them well today.

Once the engine was off and occupants had decamped, Jacob cast a glance at the van and shook his head in mock disgust. An absolute museum piece, he was genuinely surprised every time he turned the key and the battered old thing actually coughed to life.

"Ice Cream Out Loud" it read in faded colours which had once been vibrant and attractive. The name was his idea after his former business partner had emphatically vetoed the alternative *"Whippy Kye-Aye."* It was a piece of shit but had it served him dutifully. Jacob went ahead, striding purposefully toward the damaged doors before turning on his heel and addressing his companions.

"Well, here we are ladies and gentlemen; this is the place where your education will begin. Make no mistake, you are here to learn. You will listen to me, and you will do *what* I say, *when* I say. You will follow every instruction without question if you are to truly understand what we're trying to accomplish here today. You are here of your own volition. You wanted to be here, never forget that. I don't know how long we've got as they're no doubt looking for us and will probably find us eventually, so we need to work fast."

He paused for dramatic effect, then continued.

"Lessons will be learned here today, and I will be your teacher."

He heaved open the main sliding door to the old, crumbling factory unit and entered the facility with the others in tow. It was dark inside, with only the light cascading down through the many holes and cracks in the roof to guide them. As Jacob walked further into the structure, leading the group toward something which only he currently knew about, glass crunched under his feet and years of dirt and debris was kicked up in turn.

"Here we are," Jacob announced at last as he threw a previously unseen lever which resulted in sporadic, hazy, lights flickering to life overhead, many of the bulbs long since destroyed. In the centre of the factory unit directly underneath one of the few working lights was a dirty, soiled tarpaulin which had been thrown over something vaguely pyramid shaped.

"Again, remember you are here to learn, so allow me to introduce you to our specimen." Jacob pulled free the tarpaulin with all the flamboyance of a birthday magician to reveal a rickety old chair in which sat - gagged, blindfolded, and securely tied at the wrists, waist, and ankles - a young man in shorts and a vest.

"Ta-daaa!" Jacob exclaimed, leaning yet further into the magician metaphor. Although he was huffing and puffing to catch his breath with the tarp now gone but the gag still in place, the young man was clearly conscious, awake, and absolutely terrified.

"Everyone, meet Michael" Jacob said with a huge grin on his face. Bill, Sabina, and Dante's faces, however, remained fixed and unmoving at the dramatic unveiling. Jacob took their nonchalance as his cue to expand further and so continued in his elaborate performance. He held up a finger to forestall any interruptions and quickly scurried away beyond the knowing gaze of the overhead light. Back mere seconds later and pushing a serving trolley ahead of him, Jacob showed off his collection of shiny new toys to his audience. A horrifying selection of scalpels, kitchen knives, scissors, pliers, a clothes iron, hacksaws, drills, and all manner of other macabre merchandise it was too, and Jacob positively beamed with pride.

Just out of sight behind the captive Michael, Jacob had also installed a workstation stocked full with the absolute antithesis of these grizzly tools; bandages, medicines, syringes, needle and thread, intravenous drips, and even a defibrillator.

"Lesson one will commence immediately, so keep your eyes open and watch closely." He reached out toward Michael's face and snatched away the blindfold to allow his captive to see once again. Michael's eyes went wide with terror, and he watched in horror as Jacob reached for a long, serrated kitchen knife and turned to face him with blade brandished as if he were showcasing it for a TV shopping network.

Jacob took one long second to look his stricken subject up and down before deciding on *down*. He slashed Michael's right Achilles tendon with all the speed and agility of a striking cobra. Michael tried to scream out in pain, but the gag in his mouth muffled the sound. Jacob placed the knife back onto the trolley without bothering to wipe the blade clean and turned to his still-silent followers in challenge.

"Right then; who's up next?"

Michael's severed Achilles was now bandaged to prevent him bleeding out and he looked up from the chair to which he was so tightly bound and tried - eyes wide - to scream anew despite the gag. Toward him strode Dante, a dark-skinned young man in his early twenties, his face set in a determined frown and ready to follow Jacob's lead and impress his teacher. He selected a portable electronic drill from the *toy box* and he looked sidelong at Michael, weighing up his options as if selecting the best cut of meat from the butcher's counter.

Adhering to Jacob's example he lined up the shining drill-bit with Michaels right kneecap and triggered the tool to life. Dante paused momentarily to savour Michael's fear and panic and proceeded to push the spinning tool straight into the knee, breaking bone, severing muscles and tendons, and spraying blood in a bizarre spiral pattern all over the floor, all over Michael, and all over Dante. He reversed the direction of the oscillation with the flick of a switch and worked to extricate the spinning drill from the now obliterated knee. Dante grinned despite the fresh blood in his eyes; he was pleased with his work and hoped that Jacob was too.

"Go on, more!" Jacob shouted, urging Dante to go again. The student replaced the drill and selected a pair of pliers in its place before moving toward Michael's left hand which was still bound by the wrist to the chair. The wedding ring on Michael's finger had caught Dante's attention, and his eyes moved down the digit toward the nail at its tip. He took a firm hold of the fingernail with the teeth of the pliers and yanked it free of the finger before back-handing

Michael across the face with the tool still in hand, knocking him out cold.

Shit, Dante thought, *I knocked him out. We needed him awake.*

"Jacob," he said without turning to face his instructor, "I'm sorry, I didn't mean to put him out cold." Jacob did not reply immediately but paused for a moment.

"It's okay, you did well," he said at last. "Go and sit down."

Jacob was not at all concerned by Dante's enthusiasm. Quite the opposite, in fact; the boy was learning.

"Okay. So we know Dante has clearly got massive, bulging balls. The drill.... what an inspired choice," he smiled.

"What about you, old man?" he said to Bill. "Care to show a young upstart how the older generation rock and roll?"

After a few minutes in which Michael's broken and mutilated knee was bandaged up and he'd been brought back around via a combination of water, smelling salts, and a good old fashioned slap to the face, Bill was ready to take the baton in this macabre relay. Before he was allowed to perform his experiment, however, Jacob took back the reins.

"Before we go any further, allow me to proceed with lesson number two," he said, serious once more.

"I showed you a knife and Dante showed us a drill. A good start, yes, but mere surface damage nonetheless." He moved his hand back and forth above his collection of instruments as if he were selecting a chocolate bar from a shop display before deciding on a large, thin metal spike, not unlike a grandmother's knitting needle.

"If you truly want to take things to the next level, you have to go *deeper...*"

This last word was punctuated by Jacob sliding the metal spike into Michael's right ear, piercing his eardrum but going no further into his head than this. A strangled, high-pitched, almost feline whine from the gagged and bound victim was like music to Jacob's ears, and he could not help but laugh at the poor man's reaction. Taking encouragement from the suffering he was inflicting upon his specimen, Jacob casually snatched up one of the many scalpels his toy box held. Cutting the sweat and blood-soaked vest from Michael's body, he set about slicing off the man's left nipple. He flicked away his prize as if it were an expired cigarette butt, then motioned for Bill to enter the fray.

Bill was an older gentleman with liver spots beginning to show against his pale skin. He surveyed the bleeding and whimpering Michael as if approaching a Snooker table and lining up his next shot, before selecting a glinting and wicked-looking saw. He knelt in front of Michael and, without preamble, set about sawing horizontally through the lower part of his shin in order to amputate the foot and ankle below. As blood sprayed and bone cracked, Michael's muffled screams trailed off as he lost consciousness once more.

It took almost an hour this time for Jacob, after simply tossing aside the newly-severed limb, to apply a tourniquet to Michael's traumatised leg and to stabilise his vitals via the plethora of medical aids he had at his disposal.

As he slowly began to come back around to a hazy, agonising consciousness, Michael could barely hold his head up straight and instead simply allowed it to loll onto his chest as he cried softly and quietly to nobody in particular. Jacob strode slowly but purposefully into the diffuse light cast from somewhere overhead, and turned to regard his specimen.

"Not long now, my friend. Only two more lessons and you will finally be free of your pain." He pulled the bloodied, needle-like spike from Michael's ear and dropped it to the floor with a *clang*. He turned his back to the poor creature once more and addressed the room.

"Lesson three," he exclaimed as though he were projecting to a theatre audience on the opening night of an invitation-only Broadway production.

"I know this is all still new to you, but believe me when I tell you that, up until now, we have merely been *playing*." This last word he almost snarled, like a villain in a comic book.

"You came here to learn about pain; you came here to learn about suffering. So let me show you their *true* meaning."

His eyes changed. Eschewing his former ringmaster or stage actor demeanour, he became the personification of rage as he turned and struck Michael full in the face with his balled fist. Again and again he hit and struck the hapless, chair-bound soul until his nose was unrecognisable and he could only see out of one eye.

*Goo*d, Jacob thought, *as long as he* can *still see.* Jacob leaned over to his tools and picked up a large pair of industrial-grade bolt cutters. A glint in his eye, he pulled down Michael's shorts and made short work of forcibly removing the man's testicles.

Some time later, when Michael was once again bandaged up, injected with all manner of life-prolonging drugs, he opened his one remaining useful eye to behold Sabina's face a mere inch or two from his own.

He tried in vain to scream in terror.

There was a glint in her eye too, and Sabina was determined to prove to Jacob that she was ready, that she could learn. She removed the gag from Michael's mouth and found that he barely had the strength to resist as she forced his mouth open with her left hand and lined up a hammer with her right.

With a degree of force and a measure of intricacy, Sabina began bashing Michael's teeth in until they either hung in his mouth or found their way into his throat. His mouth was now a bloody, fleshy pulp, so she moved onto her next trick. Sabina took both a chisel and a hunting knife from Jacob's ghastly collection and quickly removed Michael's right eye with the former before slashing him full across the belly with the latter, opening up a sickening tear and threatening to spill the screaming man's internal organs.

She stood back in triumph and grinned a sickly grin as she beheld the fruits of her labour.

With his head thrown back and full-on belly laughing, Jacob stood before the bleeding, sobbing, barely conscious husk which had once been named *Michael* by its mother, had itself once belly-laughed whilst out drinking with its friends, trying to catch the eye of the pretty brunette by the bar; now reduced to a mere flesh and blood analogue.

"You have all performed admirably, my friends!" Jacob exclaimed with arms stretched out wide before him.

"A better class of student, I could not have wished for.

The lessons you have learned here today will serve you well for the rest of your lives, but there is still one final thing I must show you."

He reached for the same hunting knife so expertly brandished by Sabina moments earlier and took up a position behind Michael before grabbing him by the hair.

He pulled the helpless man's head back to reveal his throat - the trace of a pulse still there despite the trauma he had endured – and Jacob plunged the knife in deep. He sawed at it as if it were a loaf of bread he were carving, not a human being.

The blood was now flowing freely and openly from Michael's severed throat, so Jacob let go of the man's hair and watched as the head fell and hung low on the chest, attached to the body only by stubborn muscle and tendons at this point. He stepped back around to the front of the deceased and was startled by the sound of the front door being smashed open and the blinding lights of torches as countless were shone directly into his eyes.

"Armed police, get on the ground! Armed police, GET ON THE GROUND NOW!"

Jacob, now smiling maniacally in triumph, put his hands behind his head and dropped to his knees as the armed officers approached. From his left, he heard a young officer call to his superior.

"'Sarge! You'd better come and see this…" Once he was satisfied that Jacob was now safely in the custody of his officers, the Sergeant strode over to the younger officer and recoiled in spite of himself at the sight he beheld.

There on the floor at his feet were what looked like three Halloween masks.

The Sergeant stood and stared without word at the face of a young black man, an elderly white gentleman, and that of an Asian female in her mid-thirties, each with a piece of elastic crudely stitched to its edges to ensure a comfortable fit.

*

It didn't take long for the news reports to start flooding in.

"Police have today confirmed the arrest of forty-six-year-old Jacob Dancy for the kidnap and murder of twenty-seven-year-old Michael Williams. Williams was reported missing from his family home six days ago, and his body was recovered from the scene of the arrest.

In a macabre twist to this horrific story, police and forensic teams also recovered the remains of three other missing persons at the scene; twenty-one-year-old Nottingham university student Dante

King, sixty-seven-year-old retired I.T consultant Bill Wright from Kendal in Cumbria, and thirty-three year old shop assistant Sabina Aktar from Portsmouth. Though this has yet to be officially confirmed by police, we understand that the preserved faces of the three additional victims were worn by Jacob Dancy as masks during his prolonged and brutal attack on Michael Williams."

"We're just pausing for a moment to bring you a shocking new development in the Jacob Dancy murder case. We have just received a report which suggests that a number of small, red fibres found in the suspect's vehicle - a 1980s era ice cream van - may be linked to another crime scene in the north. You will no doubt remember that case from a few months back, in which the body of a young woman was discovered by a dog walker in a heavily wooded area, strangled and wrapped in a red carpet."

"We will of course bring you more on this as we get it."

THE FARMER'S WIFE

"So, we just want to remind you all again that you need to be extra careful. Avoid going anywhere on your own, and do not under any circumstances talk to anybody you don't know. You got it?"

"Yes Mrs. Francis," the kids of class 7b answered, with that bizarre and almost musical inflection only ever heard in classrooms.

"The most important thing to bear in mind - and I want to be absolutely clear on this - is that there's no such thing as *The Farmer's Wife*, okay? It's just a fairytale, a made-up story. It's not real. What *is* real though is that two kids from this school, from this year group, have gone missing. So, again, we all just need to be extra careful and extra vigilant, okay?"

The kids nodded their understanding and Mrs. Francis dismissed them for the day. With their coats on and their bags slung over their shoulders the kids set off for their respective homes. Some made the short walk to parents waiting in cars outside the school gates, while others made the whole journey on foot.

One of the kids walking home, Kyle, jogged to catch up with his friends Jon and Lucy halfway across the playground toward the school gates.

"She doesn't know what she's talking about," Kyle said to the brother and sister without preamble.

"What? Who?" Lucy asked.

"Mrs. Francis, of course. The Farmer's Wife is real, guys. She's totally real and she's the one who killed Lisa and Shaz," Kyle replied.

"Come on Kyle, that's not a nice thing to say. You don't even know if they *are* dead, they could just be lost or, you know, still alive," said Jon.

"Nope. They're definitely dead, and The Farmer's Wife definitely got them. I read about it online."

"Oh, so it *must* be true then," mocked Lucy.

"Laugh all you want you two, but don't come crying to me when you hear a scythe scraping along behind you, then… BANG! You're mince-meat. Just like Shaz and Lisa."

"It's not true, Kyle, so just quit it, okay? Anyway, what time are you coming round tonight?"

"Um, about six. My mom will have dinner ready, then I'll get changed and come over. Do you still want me to bring those video games?"

"Yeah, and a spare controller if you have a one," said Lucy.

With their plans now agreed, the Johnstone kids bade farewell to Kyle Wilkie as they went their separate ways home.

A few hours later, once their bellies were full and their homework was done, Jon and Lucy were sat in Lucy's room engrossed in a video game when they heard the expected knock at the door.

"It's okay mom, I'll get it," shouted Jon as he made his way downstairs to greet Kyle at the door.

"Hey man, come in," said Jon, and led Kyle upstairs.

"Hey Kyle," said Lucy, and Kyle responded in kind.

"I brought those games, dude, do you wanna…?"

"Actually," began Lucy, a ponderous look dawning on her face.

"Actually, what?" asked a confused Kyle.

"We should go play outside. It's Saturday tomorrow so we're allowed to be out a bit longer, and it's still lovely and warm out," she suggested.

"Yeah, that's a great idea Luce," her brother agreed.

"Um, I don't know guys. What about, you know, *her*?" said Kyle.

"Oh, come on, Kyle, The Farmer's Wife is not real. I can't believe you're actually buying that crap," said Jon, a little more harshly than he had intended.

"She's totally real! They say she's the vengeful spirit of a woman who was murdered hundreds of years ago. The villagers cut her throat and gouged her eyes out just to get back at her husband. Or for being a witch. Or something like that," protested Kyle.

"Get back at her husband for what?" asked Lucy.

"I don't know, some farming shit most likely. Maybe he stole their chickens or something. But she *is* real."

"So, if the villagers murdered her years ago, why would she come back now and take kids? It doesn't make any sense, Kyle. It's not real," said Jon, emphatically.

The argument seemingly settled for now, the three of them put their sneakers on and headed outside.

"Don't go too far, you three," Jon and Lucy's mother shouted after them.

"We won't," answered Lucy, fully intending to break this instruction.

They set off walking towards the wooded area not far from their house. With its narrow footpath flanked on both sides by tall trees and the sound of trickling water from an unseen stream their constant companion, it was a beautiful green spot in an otherwise grey part of the world. The sun was still warm on the backs of their necks and the trio continued forward in silence for a little while.

"Maybe they gave her a hard time," said Kyle, out of the blue.

"Huh?" replied Jon, confused.

"The kids. Maybe when The Farmer's Wife was still alive local kids gave her a hard time and that's why she takes them, especially if they thought she was a witch," answered Kyle.

"Jesus, have you been thinking about that this whole time? Is that why you were actually quiet for once?" said Lucy.

"HA-HA, very funny. But yeah, I guess I have. Think about it."

"Kyle, for the last time, she's *not real*," said Jon, holding up a hand to forestall any further argument.

They walked on in silence once more until at last they reached what appeared to Kyle to be the monstrous entrance to some sort of cave, but which turned out on further inspection to be the hollow trunk of an enormous tree, long since uprooted and now a horizontal pipe of wood and soil which receded about thirty feet into darkness.

"Isn't it cool? Go on in," said Lucy to Kyle, noting the confused look on her friend's face.

"In? In where?" he replied.

"In here, in the tree trunk," said Jon, already striding inside with a hitherto unseen plastic cigarette lighter out and glowing, guiding his way inside the dark tree trunk. Lucy gestured for Kyle to follow Jon, and she brought up the rear.

"Isn't it great?" asked Jon. "Lucy found it a few weeks back and we've been sneaking back down here to play whenever we get chance."

"Play? What can you possibly play inside a dark, wet, smelly old tree trunk? And come to think of it, what *is* that smell?" asked Kyle, wrinkling his nose at the foul aroma coming from the far end of the hollowed-out tree trunk.

"Oh, that's probably just Shaz and Lisa," said Jon, his eyes unblinking in the orange light of the flame which stood between his face and Kyle's.

"Wha-" Kyle began to ask, but his question hung unfinished in the darkness as the tip of Lucy's knife burst out through his chest.

Jon and Lucy allowed their friend to fall to his knees as the blood from his punctured organs poured openly from his torso and out of his mouth.

The brother and sister took each other by the hands, closed their eyes, and began:

"Oh, Farmer's Wife, oh Farmer's Wife,
Pray, accept our sacrifice.
With open throat and absent eyes,
Spare our souls and take your prize.

Oh, Farmer's Wife, Oh Farmer's Wife,
We offer you another life.
Reclaim your voice, reclaim your sight,
Claim this flesh and blood tonight."

Lucy knelt down beside Kyle, whose life was ebbing away fast in gouts of crimson and placed her mouth close to his ear.

"You were right, you know. She *is* real."

Kyle's eyes were fixed on the literal light at the end of the tunnel as he stared at the opening to the tree trunk, as if he could spirit himself outside to safety by sheer force of will.

As his pulse slowed and his breathing grew shallow, Kyle's vision began to darken. His senses were fading fast, and he did not have the strength to try to escape his fate.

In his last moments, just before his consciousness shrunk away to an eternal darkness, he could have sworn he heard the sound of a scythe scraping along the ground toward him.

PETER'S RABBITS

"I was born in old Virginia,
South Carolina, I did go.
There I courted a 'purty little woman,
But her age I did not know.

Well her hair was brown and curly,
Oh, her cheeks was rosy red.
On her breast she wore white lilies,
Oh, the tears that I have shed.

When I'm asleep I'm dreaming about you,
When I wake I have no rest.
Every moment seems like an hour,
Oh, the pains go through my breast.

I'd rather be in some dark 'holler,
Where the sun don't never shine.
Than for you to be some other man's darling,
When you ain't no longer mine..."

The old gramophone stood on a table in the corner, hidden in the deep shadows cast by the single bright light which hung from the ceiling of the converted basement. Peter had always loved old twenties and thirties-era records, and Clarence Ashley's 'Dark Holler Blues' was one of his absolute favourites to work along to.

As the worn, scratchy record sung out the old tune, Peter went about his work with a calm determination. His tools were already bloodied from the skinning procedure, but that was fine; he'd converted the basement for this exact reason, after all.

He had taken to keeping rabbits for the last few years now, and this one - a small, thin, black creature - was now too old to mix with the others.

So down to the basement it went.

Once the skin had finally been removed and was hanging securely on the drying rack against the soundtrack of a dusty old fiddle, Peter set about cutting up the meat.

It'll make a fine stew for the week ahead, he thought.

The skin, too, would not go to waste, and as he climbed the stairs and back onto the main floor of his modest house in the countryside, he switched off the basement light from the landing, darkening the rabbit-skin lampshade which had so effectively focused the light down onto his cold steel workstation.

Later, once the stew was bubbling away in the huge stockpot he kept aside for such exquisite dishes as this, he inhaled deeply at the myriad of aromas which his cooking had filled the house with. The mixture of spices, meat, vegetables, and a splash of red wine warmed him to the bone and instantly set his stomach off growling like a cornered animal.

He poured a tall glass of red wine for himself and sat down on the couch. As his mind wandered, he considered getting another rabbit to replace - which one did he just skin?

Mopsy, he recalled.

Yeah, I should definitely get another one, he convinced himself, nodding.

I'll catch one tomorrow, he decided.

He liked the company.

5am. He had to be up early to feed the rabbits.

Last night's wine had thus far refused to vacate his system entirely despite his relatively early night, and Peter's head was a storm of cotton wool clouds as he descended the stairs. He wasted no time in putting the kettle on and its hiss cut through the silence like an uninvited guest. Once he had made himself a strong cup of coffee, he began the practiced yet numbingly mundane task of chopping vegetables and filling bowls of water for the rabbits.

It was cold outside today, so Peter pulled his dressing gown tight around his body as he made the familiar trip outside into the morning air across the damp grass which led to the barn. His earphones were firmly ensconced beneath the raised hood of his morning robe, and he selected a Tom Waits classic from 1929 as he set about his familiar routine.

> *"When you hear sweet syncopation,*
> *And the music softly moans.*

T'ain't no sin, to take off your skin,
And dance around in your bones…"

What Peter thought of as the rabbits' hutches were actually small stables which probably housed ponies at some point. They were large enough for a grown man to step into, so were more than adequate for rabbits. He tossed the vegetables into the stalls and placed the water bowls carefully down onto the floor. Not for the first time, Peter held up a hand to forestall any attempt to escape. The rabbits tended to try and run, he had learned over the years, but he had managed to teach them to stay put. Once their daily sustenance had been provided, Peter turned his back on the three rabbits which remained now that Mopsy was no more and made his way back toward the house to shower and dress for work.

A couple of hours later, Peter opened the door to the office and was greeted by the same tired smiles and lazy waves as always. He tried to force a modicum of joviality into his demeanour and slotted himself comfortably into his chair to begin the day's menial journey into the world of sales and customer service.

Snapping him out of his revelry some hours later, Peter looked up to find James idly chatting away to him.

"…so I'll drive Mathew and Jordan, and you can jump in with John and Kristian, yeah? You can just leave your car here."

Peter was suddenly aware that he had absolutely no idea what James was talking about.

"Sorry, I zoned out for a second there. What are we doing?"

"Beers after work, you in or what?"

"Ah, no, sorry. No can do, I'm afraid. I have to duck out early tonight. I'm picking up a new rabbit." Having worked together for about three years at this point, James was more than used to Peter's idiosyncrasies but still could not stifle his laughter.

"Another rabbit? Jesus, man, how many is that now?"

"Uh, I mean, seven, I think. Since I've known you at least, big man," Peter replied, grinning.

"And you'd choose them over beers with your boys? I'm hurt. If I hadn't met Lucy last year, I'd swear you were fucking those rabbits. Sorry again about Lucy, by the way."

Lucy... Peter thought. *Now there's a story...*

"No, it's fine mate. Some women clearly don't appreciate greatness, that's all. Fuck her."

"So do you...?" James pressed.

"What?"

"The rabbits, do you fuck the rabbits?"

The pair of them broke into a fit of childish laughter which was totally unbecoming of two men rapidly approaching forty, and their miserable old cunt of a boss emerged from his office with a pointedly raised eyebrow.

How dare such wanton expressions of joviality be displayed in such a serious workplace as this? said the eyebrow.

"Well..." Peter replied in an admonished whisper "...sometimes, yeah... before I skin them."

He actually regretted turning down the offer of beers, as it had turned out to be one of those days when he could *really* have used a pint or six. Still, needs must. There was a slot to fill. He wanted another rabbit.

Peter lived out in the countryside away from the busy town centre and outlying suburbs, but he still had to pass through these densely populated areas on his way to his own, more remote home. Passing through such varied locations meant he was not short of options when it came to wildlife on his journey. Every lane, bend, nook, and turn presented new opportunities, and it wasn't long before he spotted one casually walking on the roadside, *en route* to where exactly he could only guess.

He had perfected his technique to an art form by now given the years of practice he had dedicated to the hobby. It took mere minutes for Peter to subdue and stow the rabbit away safely in his large vehicle. Excitement and adrenaline coursed through his veins and Peter could not wait to get the plump white creature back home.

He found he was not really that hungry despite a long day at work with a slow, dull hangover. Maybe it was the thought of the new rabbit in his car and the excitement this new acquisition stirred within him, but he decided he'd skip his evening meal regardless. With his work bag and coat having already been brought indoors, he went back out to the car to collect the creature and introduce it to its new home.

He made his way across the grass to the barn, passing the single wooden stake which stuck out of the ground to his right. He carried the unconscious animal in his arms and, once inside, he opened the now vacant hutch in which Mopsy had until recently resided.

Mopsy, he thought, and remembered the stew he'd made which even now sat in the fridge back at the house. The thought suddenly rendered him insatiably hungry, so he made quick work of placing the new rabbit in the cage and putting down fresh water for when it eventually awakened from its chemically induced slumber. Securing the lock, he set about placing food and fresh water into the bowls of the other rabbits, all the while ensuring they did not try to run.

They always try to run, he thought.

Once his regular nightly chores had been completed, he locked the barn and made his way back up to the house where, within the hour, he'd finished a large, hot bowl of stew and was wrapped up tight in his dressing gown watching a terrible action film to wind down his mind before bed.

He awoke the following morning bright and refreshed, ready to face another day. He had realised the previous evening that he had so far neglected to name the new arrival and toyed with the idea of simply reusing 'Mopsy'. Upon crossing the cold grass past the wooden stake and unlocking the barn, he smiled as the name came to him, inspired by James' comment the previous day.

He unlocked the cage and stepped inside and toward the rabbit. It had awoken, but was clearly frightened, confused, still a little dazed from the tranquillising cocktail of Peter's own recipe, and the creature shied away from him and backed itself into a corner.

"It's okay, Lucy, don't worry. This is your home now, okay? My name is Peter. *Peter Rabbit*, my mother always used to call me," he laughed, and the shrill, high-pitched sound echoed inside the cold wooden barn.

He placed fresh food and water onto the straw-covered floor and gently stroked the shaking rabbit's head. He backed out of the hutch, his face obscured by the thick mesh which covered the window section of the retrofitted doors and smiled at Lucy.

"I'm sure we're going to be the *best* of friends."

As he walked back toward the main barn door he fed and watered each of the other rabbits in turn. Upon reaching Flopsy's cage, he frowned and chewed his lip with his hands on his hips as he assessed the animal.

She had grown gaunt and the broken leg she had endured in her last escape attempt hadn't really healed all that well, despite his best efforts at the time.

She's not gonna last much longer, he decided.

She might have to go to the basement.

The morning's realisation about Flopsy weighed heavily on Peter's mind the whole day, despite going through the usual motions at work. He was good at his job and his colleagues considered him to be funny, charming and - at least one or two, he was acutely aware - quite handsome. But he cared nothing for them, nor their opinions.

While his physical body, his wit, his voice, and his insights were always present and available to those around him, his mind, his true self was off-limits.

Here he existed alone. His thoughts and pursuits were strictly unavailable to any but himself. Lucy - the original Lucy - had learned this the hard way. She had loved him, but he did not, perhaps *could* not, really love her back. He was like a guitar with five strings, a teddy bear with one button-shaped eye missing: here, present, but *unfinished* somehow.

She might have to go, he thought over and over.

No. She has to go.

The clock ticked inexorably onward until, at last, it was 5pm. With his workday now concluded, and drinks at the Hen-Pecked Inn refused once more, Peter drove home with purpose and resolve in place of his previous doubt and conflict. He parked the car in its usual spot and dumped his bag and laptop inside the house without finesse. He made sure to pick up his syringe as he turned on his heel and left the house as brusquely as he had entered. He didn't even bother to stop to change out of his suit and leather shoes but strode purposefully toward the barn.

Once inside, he ignored the attentions of the other rabbits and made straight for Flopsy's enclosure. The lame creature must have sensed his intentions and tried in vain to crawl away from him and toward any semblance of shelter and safety it could find. The creature's futile efforts at flight and self-preservation were no match for Peter's strength and speed as he seized the creature with one hand and injected the cocktail of drugs into its neck with the other. With the pitiful creature now rendered limp and unconscious, Peter made short work of carrying it back to the house.

He made his way down the stairs and into the basement and put Flopsy onto the cold table. Once she was safely secured atop the table, he stepped away to switch on the lights and the gramophone. He selected a record and inhaled deeply to calm his mind as the ghostly voices of singers long-since dead reached out to him from somewhere deep in the 1920s.

The music had always calmed Peter, despite the constant remarks from friends that his love of faded, dusty, scratchy old records was *weird* at best and downright *sinister* at worst.

He was in the *zone* now, and he set about his work with determination and resolve. The first task was to put the unconscious creature out of its misery, so he seized the hatchet from its usual place on from his workstation and swung down in a hard arc, severing the creature's head from its body in one powerful stroke. He allowed the blood to flow freely and unchecked, and down it went from the table into the open grate on the floor thanks to the meticulously designed drainage system he had installed into his workstation.

Once the blood had ceased flowing, he cleaned the area as best he could and set about the task of skinning the body and removing the organs and flesh which he would need for his next stew, all the while wrestling with the question of what to do with the skin once it had been dried and treated.

A belt? A pillowcase? An ornament of some kind? Fuck it, plenty of time for that later, he mused.

A few hours later he was finished. The creature had been killed, skinned, exsanguinated, and harvested for flesh and organs as required. The rest he would simply burn.

Satisfied with his work, Peter turned off the music and the lights with a nod. He went back up into the main house to place the newly harvested organs and meat into the freezer before proceeding to the shower to wash away the blood and viscera from his tired body. He ached now but resolved to grab a quick bite to eat then go straight to bed. He was aware that he hadn't fed or watered the others, but that would just have to wait until the morning.

He woke in the early hours as the answer came to him like a bolt from the blue: a case for his laptop, that's what he would do with the skin.

He was too excited to sleep much more after his early morning revelation, so he was up and alert by four. Thanks to the meticulous design and the efficiency of the appliances and systems he had installed in the basement workshop, Flopsy's skin was now mostly dry, and he couldn't wait to get started. The first thing he had to do was dispose of the bits and pieces of Flopsy which were still lying on the steel worktable. He gathered them up in a black plastic bag and carried them outside to set fire to them in a spot just a few meters back from the rabbits' shed. Somewhat ironic, to his mind.

Once the leftovers had been disposed of, he set to work tracing out the pattern for his laptop case with a thick black marker and selected his best scissors for the cutting. He was thrilled that it was a Saturday, as the flash of inspiration he had received overnight would have eaten away at his mind incessantly were he at work today.

Before too long he had cut out the stencil and had proceeded to fold and stitch like a master tailor, a practiced seamstress turning to skin upon mastering cotton. Folding, measuring, stitching, measuring again, his work was always meticulous and the plethora of lampshades, pillowcases, belts, ponchos, sheaths for his hunting knives - everything he had made from his harvested materials was a work of art.

Now it was complete, his laptop case was no different. The natural, light tone, the complimentary dark stitching, the infinitesimally precise measurements, it truly was a thing of beauty. He looked over his shoulder at the remaining strips of dried skin he still had hanging on his rack and decided to just burn those, too. He had made something special and, content with his work, had no immediate use for the skin for the time being.

Better to just harvest some more later, he concluded.

He gathered up the spare strips and took them to the still-smoldering fire he had set earlier. He tossed the skin onto the pyre and stoked the flames back to life. Once the task had been completed, he went back indoors to shower before he would finally feed and water the remaining rabbits.

I'll make it up to them, he thought. *I'll make them an extra-special breakfast and one of them may even be allowed to come inside the house for a few hours later. Lucy, maybe. Yeah, Lucy.*

Once he had showered and donned fresh clothes, Peter made his way toward the barn with a huge salad bowl full of chopped, fresh fruit and vegetables for the rabbits. It was still pretty early, and he was ready to tackle the rest of the day with a smile and a spring in his step. The sun was just daring to peek out from behind the early morning clouds and Peter could already feel its warmth on his skin.

It's gonna be a good day, he told himself.

He pushed the barn door open with one hand and proceeded to make his way along its length, feeding and watering each rabbit in turn, ignoring their pleas and cries for help.

"Please, let us go! We won't tell! Please!" screamed Lucy, whose parents had actually named her Katherine at birth.

"I just want to go home…. Please let me go…" whimpered Cotton Tail, whose face was plastered all over "Missing" posters in her hometown this very moment, the name "Eliza Jimenez" displayed prominently above the image of her delicate face.

The third remaining occupant, Benjamin, known to his friends and family as Toby Harrell, had long since given up pleading, and instead merely sat in the corner shaking in fear. Warm piss was pooling freely beneath his skinny naked body and he could feel its sting around his damaged and bleeding anus as Peter approached. The memory of Peter's *love* was still a fresh scar on his very psyche, and the emaciated teen convulsed with fear that he was going to be taken into the house again.

Peter paid them no mind and continued to systematically pour food into his pets' bowls. Once his work was done, he secured the locks on the paddocks and exited the barn which he also dutifully locked behind him. The cries and pleas receded behind him as he crossed the land between the barn and the house. On his way, Peter passed, as he always did, the solitary wooden stake which jutted upwards from a small patch of dirt.

"Morning Mom," he said out loud as he passed the mound beneath which rested all that remained of his mother.

All that remained of his mother besides his wallet and the hair inside his pillows.

Yeah, it's definitely gonna be a good day, Peter thought, grinning from ear to ear.

SLEEPING DOGS

Shlop, shlop, shlop, shlop, shlop…

Andrew flicked his wrist to activate the backlight on his smart watch - *2:20am.*

"Eddard, stop it! Go to sleep," he hissed into the darkness toward the foot of the bed. Eddard was Andrew and Kelly's pet Labrador, and Andrew had never quite gotten used to the sounds dogs tended to make when grooming, scratching, or otherwise addressing themselves. The rhythmic licking noises which had woken Andrew from his sleep ceased at the sound of his voice cutting through the darkness.

Andrew was already feeling uncharacteristically sleep-deprived of late. The recent days and weeks had seen the old house Kelly and he lived in start to demonstrate more than its fair share of strange noises. Now that winter was drawing near, the creaks, clicks, whooshes, taps, straining pipes, and other, stranger sounds had kept Andrew awake night after night. How Kelly slept through it, he simply could not understand.

And tonight, it was the turn of sloppy, licking noises it seemed.

It was still dark, and the bedroom was once again quiet at last. Andrew wasted no time in sliding right back into some semblance of sleep. Though his eyes were closed and his body was resting, his dreams were filled with disquiet and anxiety - no surprise given his exhaustion - and he could have sworn he heard a strange scratching noise coming from the foot of the bed as he drifted away toward a deeper slumber.

Shlop, shlop, shlop, shlop, shlop…

Andrew was instantly awake and once again checked his watch - 2:55am. He reached out to his left and grabbed the discarded T-shirt which lay on the floor by his bedside table, balled it up and threw it across the room toward the patch of floor at the end of the bed.

"Eddard! For fuck sake, stop it! Go to sleep!" he snapped, furious at the dog and disgusted by the sound which had woke him once more. The sound once again ceased, and silence crept back into the bedroom.

At least the dog can sleep, Andrew thought.

He on the other hand, did not fall straight back to sleep this time, but instead lay awake for over half an hour waiting for his anger and frustration to dissipate. Still Kelly slept soundly alongside him.

When sleep eventually came, Andrew was whisked away into a new dream. This time he was an active participant in his favourite comic book. He dreamed of billowing capes and evil super villains, but again there was the scratching sound, discordant, issuing from outside of his tired mind somewhere out there in the real world.

Fucking dog, he thought through the haze of his slumber.

Scratch, scratch, scratch, scratch…
4:15am.

Andrew didn't even bother to sit up this time but shouted from his prone position on the bed.

"Eddard, enough! Fucking stop it or you'll go outside!"

Now Kelly finally woke up. She sat bolt-upright in the bed and hissed at Andrew.

"What are you shouting about?"

Scratch, scratch, scratch, scratch…

"The fucking dog, laid down there scratching at something. It's bad enough that he's been licking himself all night, I can't sleep!"

Shlop, shlop, shlop, shlop, shlop…

Kelly took a moment in the darkness.

"The dog's here with me…" she replied.

Scratch, scratch, scratch, scratch…

"What?"

Shlop, shlop, shlop, shlop, shlop…

"Eddard. He's been curled up in the covers with me all night."

Stretching his right arm out toward Kelly's side of the bed, Andrew felt the familiar shape and warmth of Eddard, indeed curled up under the covers, sound asleep beside Kelly in the darkness.

Scratch, scratch, scratch, scratch. Shlop, shlop, shlop, shlop, shlop…

"Then what's making those noises…?"

ROM

"He's just not getting any better, Dev," said Priha Mahal, choking back her tears.

 "He's only ten, Pri, he'll grow out of it, he'll be okay," said her husband defiantly. Priha could hold back no longer and wept openly as she fell into her husband's arms.

The bedroom door was closed so as to spare Rom from hearing the pain in his mother's voice from his own room across the landing. There, tucked in tightly beneath his stegosaurus bedspread while his t-Rex night-light cast multi-coloured analogues of gigantic, prehistoric creatures onto his walls and ceiling, Romesh Mahal lay awake, unmoving, and unblinking. He would not sleep tonight; he never slept.

"He thinks he's dead, Dev," Pri managed through her tears. "Our baby boy thinks he's dead."

To say that Rom had difficulty making friends would be an understatement, and as he sat by himself in Mrs. Sullivan's year six class watching two birds flutter around merrily in the huge tree outside of their classroom window, he paid no attention to his classmates nor to his teacher.

"Rom? Rom. Hey, are you listening?" said Mrs. Sullivan, nicely but firmly, as she wanted his attention but was all-too aware of

Rom's apparent emotional problems. Rom slowly turned his head back toward the classroom, leaving the birds to their dance and bringing his classmates and teacher back into focus once more.

"Yes." he said in answer to Mrs. Sullivan's question.

"Okay, good; so what's the answer?"

Rom's eyes narrowed slightly, and he regarded his teacher with a fixed stare.

"I do not know," he said, truthfully.

"I do not know…" said Timmy Jenkins in a mocking imitation of Rom's accent and monotone delivery.

"Okay, hey, that's enough," said Mrs. Sullivan, struggling to be heard over the laughter which had erupted at Timmy's interjection.

"Settle down, all of you. Okay now. Rom: do you remember what I told you before about paying attention?"

"Yes," he replied, offering nothing further.

"I think he needs an oil change, maybe someone should try turning him off and on again," Timmy offered, sending the whole class into hysterics once more.

"Right! That's enough. Timmy, you…" the teacher began, but Rom was already out of his chair and striding purposefully toward the other boy. Without breaking his stride, he grabbed Timmy by the hair and slammed the boy's face down onto his desk.

Timmy cried out in pain as his nose broke with a loud crack, and blood stained both his face and his desk. Mrs. Sullivan ran through the now-silent rows of kids and took Rom firmly by the shoulders and began to lead him out of the classroom. She turned to Sally Duffy - one of the good kids - and pointed at Timmy.

"Sally, get him to the nurse. The rest of you sit tight, I'll be back in a moment."

"Hello? Yes, this is Mr. Dev Mahal, who am I speaking to?"

Already exhausted from the late-night conversation with Pri and the ensuing hour trying to soothe and reassure her, the call Dev received at work was the *last* thing he needed.

"Oh, Mrs. Sullivan, hi. Is everything…. oh… he did *what*? Are you sure it was… okay, *okay*. I'll be right there."

Dev placed his mobile down onto his desk and closed his eyes. He could hear a myriad of conversations going on around him as the team he managed worked their way enthusiastically through their data - *not making calls but making friends*, he always said - but it was all a blur to him. He rubbed at the bags which were showing more and more under his eyes these days, as if doing so would erase them and restore some energy to his flagging body.

He inhaled deeply, opened his eyes, and picked up his phone. Standing up from his desk and leaving his office, he smiled at his team, gave them a collective thumbs-up and made for *his* manager's office, where he knocked on the door and entered in one motion.

"Patricia, I'm so sorry; I have to go," he held his mobile phone aloft as if doing so would validate his claim somehow.

"That was Rom's school, I have to go."

Patricia was a tough boss, not the sort to take bullshit from anybody, and certainly not the sort to accept a *headache* or an *upset stomach* as reason to call in sick the night after a football match or birthday party. She'd been around the sales game long enough to see straight through those old tricks. But she was not without heart and, in Dev's defence, the concern and fear he felt was etched upon his face for all to see.

"What's happened? Is he okay?" she asked immediately.

"He's fine, but there's been an… incident," Dev replied, the beginnings of a tremble threatening his lower lip no matter how hard he fought it. Patricia did not fail to notice it.

"Go, it's okay. Just keep me posted, okay?"

He had arrived at the school within half an hour and was now leading Rom out of the front gates and toward his waiting car, having been filled in on the whole story by both Mrs. Sullivan and the school's headmistress.

"Come on buddy, in you get," Dev said kindly, helping his son into the car and securing his seatbelt. Rom stared at the seatbelt fastened securely around his waist and shoulder then turned his gaze upon his father. With a very slow and very slight shake of his head, he spoke to his father as if *he* were the parent and *Dev* the ten-year-old.

"You know this makes no difference," was all he said before turning to face forward, stony faced once more.

Dev loved his son, loved him with all his heart. He and Pri had tried for years to conceive a baby but had found that they could not, at least not naturally. The IVF had failed spectacularly, too, so they had but one remaining alternative.

Yes, Dev loved his son with everything he had, but sometimes Rom scared the living shit out of him.

Dev and Pri had decided not to go with the nuclear option on Rom, as they knew that children like him did not respond well - if they even responded at all - to screaming and shouting. They still wanted, *needed*, to get to the bottom of his actions though, so the softly-softly approach it was. The three were seated around the dinner table enjoying their evening meal when Pri decided the time was right to press her boy for a little more information.

"Hey, Romesh," began Pri. "What were you learning with Mrs. Sullivan this morning? You know, before you came home?"

Rom looked up at her with a face which might as well have been a cheap plastic Halloween mask for all the emotion it betrayed.

"Numbers. I'm good at numbers," he said, before turning his attention to his meal once more.

"Yes, you are, you're a smart boy, Rom. And do you know why you got to come home early today?"

"Yes."

"Well?" his mother pressed, hoping for a more detailed response.
"Can you tell me why?"

Romesh placed his cutlery onto the table beside his plate and looked up at her once more. He paused for a moment and tilted his head a little, as if carefully considering his response.

"Because Timmy Jenkins is a cunt," he said, picking his knife and fork back up. His parents sat open mouthed, barely able to comprehend the words their son had so casually spoken. It was Dev who broke the stunned silence.

"Romesh! Where did you learn such foul language? Go to your room, right now! You have gone too far, child!" he bellowed at his son.

Rom stood up, turned on his heel, and took himself upstairs as instructed, leaving his father dumbstruck and his mother wiping away the betraying tear which had rolled slowly down her cheek during her husband's outburst. There they both sat in stunned silence until Dev issued a noise which was half exasperation and half exhaustion as he placed his forearms and forehead onto the dinner table.

A few hours later, Rom was in bed with his night-light projecting the usual vivid colours onto his bedroom walls and ceiling whilst, across the hall, his parents hissed under their breaths and gesticulated wildly.

"He broke his nose, Pri! He broke another child's fucking nose! We're lucky the parents aren't pursuing this further. And that language…"

"I know, Dev, I know, but he's still our boy. Regardless of how different he is, we can't give up on him."

She looked down at her hands before adding quietly, almost to herself, "I won't give up on him." Dev saw the torment on his wife's face and took her hands in his own.

"We're not giving up on him, Pri, but he needs help. He needs some serious fucking help. I think we should take him to see a child psychologist. I've been doing some research online, and there's a place in town we can take him."

Priha agreed, though reluctantly at first, and Dev wasted no time in emailing the child psychologist whose details he had actually been sitting on for a while now, though Pri didn't need to know that part.

Just in case, he had told himself over and over.

Just in case.

Later that night, once the decision had been made and the email had been sent despite the lateness of the hour, all was quiet in the midnight darkness of the Mahal household. Pri and Dev slept in the master bedroom whilst Rom lay awake as ever in his room across the way. Dev's dreams were a torrid, tormented affair which he would not remember come morning, and his tossing and turning was preventing both he and Pri from getting any meaningful, deep sleep. This would perhaps explain why both Pri and Dev awoke so easily when they heard the *creak* coming from their bedroom door. Sitting up in bed as one, the pair looked toward the thin slice of light which now shone into their room from the landing. Stood within the sliver of the opened doorway and silhouetted against the electric light, Rom stood stock-still and just waited there, staring at his parents with a stuffed stegosaurus in hand.

"Rom? What are you doing?" asked Dev, groggily.

"What time is it? Go back to bed."

Rom stood and stared a moment longer. But for his parents, meeting his fixed gaze in the near darkness, the moment felt like it could easily have been a day or even a week.

"It's okay," Rom said at length. "Don't worry. Go back to sleep. I'm not really here anyway."

He did not move, and his parents did not ask him to again. The fear they felt at his disturbing words and unfaltering stare seemed to paralyse them, and both Pri and Dev simply laid back down as their son had instructed.

It would not be Rom alone who did not sleep that night.

Dev took a deep breath and forced a smile as he called Patricia early the following morning. With an entirely false and wholly unconvincing upbeat tone in his voice, he explained to his boss that he would not be able to go in to work as he had "things" - as he put it, far too casually - to sort out where Rom was concerned.

"Dev, is everything okay? You know you can speak honestly with me. Is Rom okay?" she asked, not buying his jovial dismissal of the facts one iota.

"Yeah, he's fine, we're all absolutely fine. We just have to take him to an appointment, that's all," Dev replied, his heart devoid of the saccharine with which his words dripped so freely and so falsely.

"Okay, Dev," replied Patricia flatly, still unconvinced. "Take a few days, and we'll just see you on Monday."

Dev thanked his boss and hung up, breathing a huge sigh of relief at the gift of a few days holiday, whether enforced or not. Pri had already made a similar call, excusing herself from her work commitments for a few days, too. Both Pri and Dev were generally happy at work. They were good, hardworking employees with thoughtful and obliging employers, and they knew they were fortunate in this respect.

Within a few hours the trio were in Pri's car and en route to the hastily arranged appointment with child psychologist Dr Moran. Neither Pri nor Dev spoke much during their twenty-minute journey, and Rom simply sat in the back and stared forward with never a word uttered. Once inside the brightly lit and colourfully decorated offices, they took a seat in the waiting room but were not made to wait long. Dr Moran called them within a few minutes, and offered each of the Mahals a drink which none of them accepted.

"So, you must be Rom. I'm Dr Moran, it's nice to meet you," the kindly doctor said to Romesh, extending her hand toward him by way of greeting. Like the earlier offer of juice, the hand was declined. Dev had already explained Rom's issues to the doctor prior to meeting in person, so there was no imperative to discuss anything of the sort today in front of the boy. As the minutes went by, the doctor continued to press Rom on various subjects in a practiced attempt to get him to open up, to share his thoughts, to actually speak more than one or two words at a time if at all possible. So far, she had achieved very little, so decided to try a different approach.

"Hey, Mum, Dad?" she began, fixing them with a look which said much more than her actual words betrayed.

"Did you see our new break room when you came in? You didn't? Oh, it's great, we have *so* much cool stuff in there now. Why don't you two go take a look and me and Rom can talk some more, okay?"

Wavelengths in sync, Pri and Dev obliged and left the doctor and Rom together while they went to *check out the cool new break room.* In doctor Moran's defence, the new break room *was* pretty impressive. Kitted out with brand new tea and coffee machines, modern fixtures and fittings, reading materials to peruse and even an Xbox for the kids to play on while their parents discussed their problems in the language of furtive glances and euphemisms. It was currently empty save for Dev and Pri.

"She seems nice," Dev offered whilst inputting their choices into the coffee machine.

"Yes. What do you think they're talking about in there, Dev? I don't like leaving them alone like this."

Dev had expected this reaction from his wife, as he felt the exact same way. Still, Dr Moran was a professional, so they had to trust that she knew what she was doing.

"You know what it's like, Pri. It's sometimes easier for kids to open up if their parents aren't around. I don't think it's anything more than that, just creating a safe environment for him, you know?"

"I know. But Rom's not like other kids, Dev, you know that."

He *did* know that. He knew that more than he would ever admit to anyone, even Pri.

"Let's just sit and drink our coffee, huh? I'm sure he's fine."

Pri conceded the point to her husband, and they sat and drank their coffee in silence, waiting impatiently as Dr Moran continued to talk to Rom.

"I like your t-shirt, Rom, is that a pterodactyl?" the doctor asked, pointing to the flying dinosaur on Rom's top. He looked down as if to check before meeting her eyes once more.

"Yes," he confirmed.

"Well, it's very cool. So, you like dinosaurs, huh?"

Rom considered this for a few seconds.

"No. Not really," he concluded.

"Okay," replied the doctor enthusiastically, hoping that some of her energy would rub off on the child. "What do you like? Sports? Video games? Comic books?"

Again, Rom seemed to consider the question for a few moments before responding.

"I like the nighttime. And I like to think," he offered, and Dr Moran was quick to seize upon this thread.

"I like to think, too. I find it relaxing. What do you like to think about, Rom? Do you think about your Mum and Dad?"

"Yes."

"Do you have fun with your Mum and Dad, Rom? Are they nice to you?"

"I think they are afraid of me."

"Are you afraid of *them*? Rom, have your Mum or Dad ever made you sad? Have your Mum and Dad ever hurt you?"

Had Pri and Dev been present for this portion of the session, they would have grasped the subtext of this particular line of inquiry immediately and likely been horrified by the direction this conversation was beginning to take.

"No. They have never hurt me. I don't think they can," Rom answered, not taking his eyes off Dr Moran for a second.

"Why do you think that?" she asked.

"Because I don't exist. Because you can't hurt somebody who's already dead."

Dr Moran was more grateful for her experience and training at that point than at any other time in her career to date, as she was able to hide the horror she felt at Rom's response. She did not cover her mouth with her hand, she did not shiver or recoil from his cold words or his unwavering stare but kept her composure and kindly veneer.

"Rom, honey, why do you say that? You know that you're here with me right now, don't you? So you do exist, see? You're not dead, Rom. You're here. You're alive. You didn't die, Rom."

"Thank you. That's a nice thought. I only wish it were true," he replied, sounding more like a world-weary adult than a ten-year-old.

"But I never said I *died*, doctor. I never existed in the first place. I am not here."

Now the doctor could not hold back the tide of dread which had started in the pit of her stomach and was now spreading through her like a raging forest fire.

He couldn't be... Surely he's not... she thought aghast, unwilling to finish the thought.

"Hey, Rom, I have a cool game: quick-fire questions, okay? Great, okay, so: What's the capital of Papua New Guinea?"

"Port Moresby."

"What's the atomic number of Zinc?"

"Thirty."

"What's three thousand, seven hundred and twenty-five, multiplied by seven thousand, eight hundred and twenty-six?"

"Twenty-nine million, one hundred and fifty-one thousand, eight hundred and fifty, doctor."

"Okay honey, we're gonna get your parents back now."

Within a few minutes Pri and Dev were back in the consultation room, trying not to read too much into the dark look on Dr Moran's face. Rom remained as expressionless and unreadable as ever and merely sat still with his hands on his lap, staring forward relentlessly.

"Okay, so it was great to meet you, Rom. I'm just going to grab a quick word with your Dad a second, okay honey? It was lovely to meet you too, Mrs. Mahal," said the doctor, standing up and extending her hand to politely dismiss mother and son. Once they had left, the doctor's mask slipped and she turned a fiery, no-bullshit gaze on Dev, freezing him in place.

"Mr. Mahal, I'm only going to ask you this once…" she said without preamble, and put her theory to Dev. He did not answer verbally but simply nodded, lending some artificial force to the tears which were now falling openly from his tired eyes. The doctor, however, had no sympathy for the emotional wreck of a man who stood in front of her.

"Fuck you. *Fuck you*, Mr. Mahal. You should have told me! How dare you put me in this position without all the facts? I can't help you. I'm not equipped to deal with…. well, to deal with kids like Rom.*"*

"Please!" begged Dev, knowing what was coming. "Please, you have to help us! Just a few more sessions, and then I can…"

"No, absolutely not," she interjected unapologetically. "I can't see Rom anymore. I won't. You know where you need to go, Mr. Mahal. You know what you need to do."

Dev *did* know, of course. He knew exactly where he needed to go and exactly what he needed to do. Once he was back at the car, he found his wife and son already strapped in tight and waiting for him. Pri did not fail to notice her husband's puffy red eyes and closed her own in understanding and resignation. She took her phone out of her pocket and typed two words before turning it slightly so that Dev could see the screen.

Professor Shore? it read.

Dev gave one short, curt nod in confirmation and Pri pursed her lips tight to keep from crying in front of Rom.

They hadn't seen Professor John Shore in ten years, and they had always hoped they would never have cause to see the man again.

New clients, it turned out, had to languish at the bottom of a long waiting list before they were granted a consultation with Professor Shore. Returning clients, however, were able to jump to the top of the list and see the man within a day or two, a fact which had rankled Pri and Dev all those years ago but had them counting their lucky stars today as they pulled up outside the building. They each took a calming breath, affected smiles which did not carry to their eyes, and unbuckled their seatbelts.

"Come on, honey. It's time to go see Professor Shore, okay?" Pri said to Rom as she opened the back door to extract the boy. Rom nodded his understanding but did not speak in reply. They made their way up the steps and into the impressive looking building full of modern, sleek lines. All steel and glass, it was truly a triumph of modern architecture.

In stark contrast to the decor, however, were the building's other *visitors*. Once Dev and Pri had signed in at reception and were making their way to their designated location, they passed a multitude of other couples, either here by themselves or with a child in tow. They passed countless adults and children on their way to Professor Shore's consultation room, but not a single smile did they encounter.

This is a bad place, thought Pri as they walked, trying not to make eye contact with anybody. The distinction between the impressive architecture and its broken occupants was a stark and disquieting contrast which made Pri think of a documentary she had once seen about a hospital ward for terminally ill children, and the multitude of bright colours and imaginative designs in which its occupants were cruelly fated to breathe their last.

They were called in to see the Professor with little time to wait and were struck by the man's appearance and demeanour. He was at least three stone heavier than he had been the last time their paths had crossed, and his hair had all-but disappeared too. His manner, however, was the same. Professor Shore was a *confident* man. Some would call it arrogance, while others would perhaps suggest he merely had the utmost belief in his own abilities, harbouring zero doubts as to his own talents.

"Dev, Pri! It's been a long time," he said, shaking each hand in turn with a genuine smile on his face. He squatted down in spite of his size and looked Rom in the eye.

"And little Rom, I see. Fascinating."

He stood up with an audible sigh and he turned his attention once more to Dev and Pri.

"So, I understand you've been having problems. My assistant said Rom doesn't sleep, is that right?"

"Yes. He barely closes his eyes, Professor. And he, um… he…" Dev struggled to articulate his concerns, but Professor Shore was already aware and nodded along in understanding.

"He thinks he's dead, yeah-yeah-yeah, I know." he said, waving a hand in casual dismissal. It startled Dev and Pri a little that he could be so flippant about the subject, especially in front of Rom himself.

"Okay," he continued, with a single clap of his hands, "let's see what we're dealing with, shall we?"

He gestured toward the medical examination table on the right-hand side of the consulting room and Pri lifted Rom up to sit him on it as instructed. Rom's legs dangled over the edge and his back was to the professor.

"Okay, here goes," said Shore, picking up a small, thin screwdriver.

"Hey, Mum," the Professor said to Pri, "why don't you tell Rom a story, huh? Keep his attention on you for a minute, okay?"

Pri nodded and forced back a tear which was threatening to make an untimely appearance at the corner of her eye.

"Hey Rom? Baby? Did I ever tell you the story of the lost little duckling? No? Okay, well. Once upon a time, there was a little duckling. It was a beautiful, sunny day and he was walking along happily with his mummy and his brothers and sisters…"

Professor Shore inserted the screwdriver into a barely visible nook in the back of Rom's head and began to turn it, slowly and precisely.

"…he loved being outside with his family, and he was happy. Just then, the little duckling saw a bright, shiny penny laying in the road. Forgetting his brothers and sisters for a moment, he waddled over for a closer look. When he got there, he realised that it wasn't a penny at all, but just a crumpled milk bottle lid…"

The Professor placed the newly removed screw between his teeth and set about removing the second.

"…he was disappointed that it wasn't a real penny, so the little duckling turned to go back to his family. But they were no longer there. They hadn't noticed he had waddled away and had continued on their way without him. He was sad, scared, and he started to cry. "Come back to me" he quacked, but nobody could hear him..."

"Almost got it..." said the Professor, more to himself than anybody else.

"The little duckling was lost, and he wished more than anything that his mummy and his brothers and sisters would come back and find him. The day began to turn dark as clouds blocked out the sun, and the little duckling cried. He was so, so alone. All of a sudden, just as the rain began to fall, he heard his mummy's voice through the darkness. "Come back to me, little duckling, come back to me" she quacked..."

"Got it," said the Professor, as he removed the second screw and the panel on the back of Rom's head along with it. He pushed the tip of his finger inside ever so slightly, and Pri and Dev winced at the audible *click* as the springs ejected Rom's motherboard.

The light immediately went out of the boy's eyes.

The Professor turned the board over in his hands, scrutinising the chips and connections in a bid to ascertain the problem.

Dev remained where he had been the whole time, stood in the corner of the room staring at the floor and Pri now wept openly, looking into her son's motionless face and newly darkened eyes.

"Come back to me, little duckling," she whispered to herself through the tears.

"Aha, here we go," said Shore. "One of the chips is damaged, you see, here? Yeah, that would explain its behaviour." He nodded to himself and smiled, happy with his diagnostic.

"Gimme a few minutes and I'll repair it for you."

Dev had not yet looked up from the floor, and Pri was still staring into Rom's dull, motionless face, her own countenance a mask of pain and torment.

"No," she said, meekly.

Professor Shore looked up from his workbench.

"Excuse me?"

"No," Pri repeated, finding her voice this time.

"Pri..." Dev began, slowly shaking his head, but his wife was now on her feet and wiping away her tears with the back of her hand.

"No, Dev. I can't.... I just can't do it anymore."

"Pri, think about what you're saying, that's our son you're talking about," Dev tried to reason.

"No, Dev. It isn't. It never was. I just can't do it anymore"

*

Dev and Pri did not speak, nor did they hold hands as they left. They tried not to look at the faces of the other parents in the waiting room and did not look back as they exited the *John Shore Institute for Bio-Robotics and Engineering,* two leaving where three had entered.

Dev started the car in silence and Pri forced herself to cast a glance into the rearview mirror, some form of silent penance to her mind. She forced down the grief which threatened to choke her as she saw the stuffed stegosaurus laying on the otherwise-empty back seat. She returned her gaze forwards, to the road and to the future, with her own words still ringing in her ears.

Come back to me, little duckling…

OF CHRISTMAS PAST

Evelyn and Christian had come a long way these last few years, but Christmas was still hard for them. Just making it to their early thirties alive was something their respective families had not expected, given the addictions they had struggled with since their teens. Clean now, gainfully employed, and heading down a better, more hopeful road, they had a great deal to be thankful for. No accomplishment nor milestone, however, could fill the void in their lives which had opened the day they had given little Noel up for adoption.

They could not have kept him, not in the state they were in; still only kids themselves, hooked on drugs, and well-known to the Police, raising a child was simply out of the question. Giving up their baby, whilst undoubtedly the right thing to do, had led them deeper still into their vices as they struggled to process their experiences. Ultimately though, the very act which had caused them to spiral had also been their salvation, as each passing year chipped away at their juvenile delinquent personas to reveal the caring, thoughtful adults they had hoped to one day become.

As was their tradition, they had settled early on Christmas eve, and were dressed in new pyjamas and matching novelty slippers. They were warmed in equal parts by the open fire at their backs and the mulled wine in their hands, and as it was Christmas Eve, they would each select one small present from the pile to open before inevitably enjoying another glass or two of the hot, spicy drink and then retire to bed.

"So we don't disturb Santa" as Evelyn always said.

Their routine was much like that of a thousand other couples out there, but one thing perhaps unique to them was the ritual of pouring a third glass for Noel and leaving it on the mantle until Christmas morning, when Christian would quietly take it away and pour it out while Evelyn watched on with glistening eyes.

The three customary glasses had been dutifully poured, and the present selection process was well underway. Evelyn and Christian's smiles turned to frowns as they heard a knock at the front door. Their respective families long-since estranged, they shared a momentary look of confusion before Evelyn stood up to answer the knocking. *Carol singers, great*, she thought, opening the door in her Santa Claus PJs and elf slippers. A teenage boy and girl in festive scarves, jumpers, and woolly hats were all smiles as they begun without preamble.

"Ding dong merrily on high…." Evelyn had to hand it to them, they could hold a tune.

"…Hosanna in excelsis!" they eventually finished.

"Yay, well done! That was great, you two!" said Evelyn, smiling and clapping. "I don't have any money to give you, but here…" she said, handing them each a Christmas cracker and a mince pie from the hallway table.

"Thanks so much, ma'am" the young girl said in response.

"Yeah, really, you didn't have to; we sing for Jesus, not for reward." added the boy.

"Oh, well, in that case: *God bless you*. Merry Christmas!"

Evelyn closed the door and went back inside to her Husband, who was squeezing and shaking presents in an attempt to discern their mysterious contents.

"They gone?" he asked.

"Be nice! I think they were from the Church; nice kids".

Evelyn had knelt down next to Christian and resumed the present picking, when another knock at the door had her on her feet again.

*What now? s*he thought, approaching the door. Opening it, she beheld the same carol singing boy from moments earlier.

"I'm so, so sorry, ma'am, I really hate to have to ask, but is there any chance I could quickly use your bathroom? It's a long way back to the Church Hall, and…"

Evelyn would not ordinarily entertain the idea, but he seemed like such a wholesome young man; and he really *did* look like he was about to burst.

"Well, it *is* Christmas. Come on in - what was your name?"

"Oh, thank you, thank you so much. And it's Luke, like in the Bible. My friend's name is actually Mary, if you can believe that." he added, smiling.

"Just down the hall and to your right, Luke."

Christian's outstretched arms and raised eyebrows were met with a stern look from Evelyn, immediately forestalling his protest.

"Be. Nice." she whispered.

A few minutes later, Luke returned to the living room looking *relieved*, to say the least.

"Better?" Christian asked.

"Oh yes, much! Thank you, sir." replied the boy, making no effort to leave, but instead looking around the festively decorated living room.

"This is a lovely house you guys have here" he said, earnestly.

"Oh, thank you Luke. We like it." Evelyn replied.

"Nice place to raise a family; do you guys have kids?"

"No, no kids."

"Oh, that's too bad. Maybe one day, huh, Evelyn?" Luke said, smiling.

Evelyn and Christian felt a simultaneous chill at the back of their necks.

"How do you know my name? Do we know each other?" she asked.

"Hm? No, you must have told me." the boy replied, still smiling.

"I didn't tell you my name." said Evelyn, alarm and concern beginning to seep into her blood.

"I must have heard Christian say it then".

"How do you know *my* name? What the fuck is this?" Christian replied.

Luke stood still, unblinking, his earnest smile fading into something infinitely more malicious.

"Oh boy. Now I've done it." he said, mostly to himself.

"Where's your friend Luke; where's Mary?" Evelyn asked, suddenly concerned for the girl.

"She's gone."

"Gone where? Back to the Church?"

"No. Just gone. As a matter of fact, she's just in the alley behind your house."

"What did you do, Luke?"asked Christian.

"She was no longer useful to me, so I got rid of her. But you two would know all about that, wouldn't you?"

The boy's once wholesome face was now a mask of rage and malevolence.

"Who the fuck are you? What's going on?" demanded Christian.

"Please don't raise your voice to me, *Dad*."

Horror and disbelief etched themselves into Christian's face, and he stared at the boy for what seemed like an eternity.

"N…. *Noel*?"

"That's right." said the boy. Without warning, he pulled a handgun out from under his colourful Christmas jumper and put three bullets into his Father's chest, adding two more to his head for good measure.

"Don't you fucking move!" he screamed at a distraught Evelyn, whose fight or flight instinct had decided on the latter course of action the second she saw the weapon.

"Why? Why are you doing this?" she managed through the tears and panic.

"You made me go away." Noel responded calmly.

"I was an inconvenience to you, so you made me go away. Do you have any idea what it's been like for me? Did you ever even try to find me? To check in on me? The things I've…"

He stopped short, and took a long, deep breath to compose himself.

"It's taken me a long time to find you." he said, and shot his mother in both legs.

Evelyn hit the deck hard, screaming, losing blood, and lying inches from her dead husband. Even without the gunshot wounds, the shock and horror of the previous few minutes would have rendered her incapable of fighting off Noel, who had now straddled her and was sitting on her chest, pinning her in place.

So distraught and frightened was she, that she did not even see him pull the knife from its sheath and only became aware of it when the cold steel blade pierced her throat in the first of many strokes to come.

The frenzied attack was soon over, and Noel's mother and father lay dead at his feet. He ran a bloodied hand through his hair then replaced his weapons. He stood for a long moment and surveyed the scene, nodding slowly to himself as he assessed his handiwork.

At length, he walked over to the mantle, garishly decorated as it was in all manner of Christmas ornaments. He helped himself to the conspicuous glass of mulled wine which stood there invitingly, and he drank deep, savouring every last drop.

He wiped his mouth with the back of his hand, smearing his mother's blood across his face in a hellish approximation of a carnival clown's smile, and threw the empty tumbler to shatter in the open fireplace, then turned around to take one final look at his dead parents.

"Merry fucking Christmas."

HALL OF MIRRORS

The *St Christopher's Crazy Carnival* came around this time every year. It would roll into town just after the holidays when the skies were still dark by late afternoon and you could smell the cold in the air, but this was the first time Selina and Phoebe had attended. When they were younger, their respective parents had never allowed them to go, as they had been told time and time again that those kinds of places were breeding grounds for *'weirdos and kidnappers'*. By the time they'd reached their teens they simply didn't *want* to go, as the whole idea seemed childish to them. With age, however, comes a change of perspective, and the now twenty-seven-year-old lifelong friends found themselves walking and laughing among the rows of attractions, rides, games, and - of course - crowds.

Probably all weirdos and kidnappers, Selina thought absently, raising a grin that she barely registered. They had stood in line to fail miserably at games of skill and had waited longer still for their turn on the waltzers, and they were starting to tire as the night went on.

"Come on Pheebs, we should probably think about heading back," said Selina, stifling a yawn.

"Oh, come on Selina, just a few more rides. How often is it just us these days, huh, away from the guys?"

She had a point, of course. They were grown women now and each living with their respective partners; all work and no play, at least not like it was when they were younger.

"Okay, you got me. Kasper and JJ will just have to miss us a bit longer," Selina responded, and both girls laughed as Phoebe leaned in and linked arms with her best friend. They walked a little further in silence until Phoebe spotted something ahead and made Selina jump a little with her sudden exclamation.

"Oh! Look! The Hall of Mirrors! Let's do that one…" and she set off at a jog, dragging her friend along behind her. Phoebe ran toward the attraction and Selina dutifully followed, but once they were inside, she let out an exasperated sigh.

"Hall of Mirrors, really? These things are so lame. Look, we're literally the only ones in here."

"Don't be a dick, Sel, come on," replied Phoebe, moving further inside the maze of mirrors. Selina followed her and had to admit she was amused by the distorted analogues she passed, each one gazing back at her in its own unique way. One was stretched tall and thin, towering over her usual diminutive height. Another was squashed and round like she'd swallowed a huge beach ball or something equally ridiculous. Phoebe had gone on ahead, but Selina was in no rush to race after her, and instead took her time passing her surreal, inverted counterparts. For a moment or two Selina allowed herself to imagine that they were in fact real beings trapped behind crystal and staring back at her from some alternate plane of existence. Tall, short, thin, wide, wavy, twisted; each subsequent reflection presenting a different Selina. Similar, but *different*.

She walked on further, lost in her own wild imagination, when she suddenly came to a stop, her breath catching in her throat and her heart skipping a beat. Amidst the unlikely, ungainly distortions which surrounded her on all sides, was a perfectly normal reflection.

They must have installed a normal mirror by mistake, she thought, waving her hand back and forth slowly and seeing her inversion do likewise.

"Hey, Selina, you there? Come on, let's get a hotdog," came Phoebe's voice from somewhere ahead of her. Looking back at her perfectly normal reflection, Selina laughed under her breath.

I told her it was lame, she thought, now ready to leave and head home.

"Yes, you did," said her reflection.

Selina inhaled sharply and threw her hands up over her mouth and noted in horror that her reflection did not follow suit.

"You told her, but she did not listen to you. She *never* listens to you."

"What the fuck is this? What the fuck is going on? Who are you?" Selina stammered.

"I am you. Well, sort of," said the reflection. "I am what you *could* be, what you *should* be. I am what you really *want* to be," it said, a cruel smile pulling at the corners of its mouth and eyes.

"No, no… this isn't real, this is not real," Selina said, the panic she felt somehow not reflected by the mirror-being she beheld not three feet in front of her.

"Oh, it's real, Selina. I can assure you of that," the creature in the mirror replied.

Selina looked left and right, looked behind her and, shaking her head in denial, made to leave.

"And where do you think you're going?" mirror-Selina asked.

"I…I… home, I… I've got to go home."

"But I haven't told you why I'm here yet. Surely you'll at least stay for that?" the thing in front of her pleaded.

When Selina neither responded nor made any attempt to leave, the mirror-being smiled.

"Good… I thought you'd want to know. But, then again, you *already* know, don't you? You know what you have to do."

"I… I… No, no no no, I won't. I won't do it."

"Say it, Selina, say it. Tell me what you have to do, and I will let you go," said her reflection. Selina stood for a moment that felt like an eternity, but she finally found her voice.

"I… I have to kill them. I have to kill them both," she admitted to the thing in the mirror.

"There you are! Come on, we'd better go, huh?" said Phoebe, coming back around the corner and taking Selina's arm once more.

"That was fun! I told you the Hall of Mirrors isn't lame," she said.

"Huh? Oh, yeah, I guess," replied Selina, confused and unsettled by the emergence of the sentient reflection which, when she looked again, was gone, replaced by an inverted, wonky analogue more suited to the rest of the attraction.

"Hey," said Phoebe, stopping to take a closer look at her friend. "Are you okay?"

"Huh? Oh, yeah. Sorry. I just…" Selina stopped mid-sentence, unwilling or unable to speak the words her mind suggested.

I just need to kill you, she thought.

"You just *what*, Selina? What's going on, have you taken something?"

Selina didn't answer, at least not in words, but within a second, she was on top of Phoebe, straddling her prone friend, hands tight around her throat and squeezing with all her strength. Within a few minutes, Phoebe had ceased struggling, and lay still and slack beneath Selina's hands, eyes bulging and tongue hanging out of her mouth. Selina remained in place for a further few minutes, slowing her breath, regaining control of her pulse and heartbeat. She had killed Phoebe, her best friend, her lifelong ally and confidante, yet she did not shed a tear.

Instead she stood and took a long, deep breath, straightened her hair and clothing, and turned on her heels to leave the Hall of Mirrors alone by the same door she and Phoebe had entered together what now felt like a lifetime ago.

Selina walked straight back through the carnival and toward the waiting comfort of her car. Getting in and securing her seatbelt, she set off calmly for home where she knew Kasper was waiting for her, probably still awake despite the lateness of the hour. She drove in silence, leaving the radio off and devoting her attention entirely to the blackness of the road ahead of her and the night into which it inexorably stretched.

It was not long before she reached the modest home which she had shared with Kasper for nearly four years at this point, and upon trying the door she found it was unlocked.

He's still up, she thought. *Good.*

"Hey, I'm back," she called as she entered the house and locked the door behind her.

"Hey. Did you have fun?" Kasper shouted back somewhat distractedly from the direction of the living room.

Probably playing video games, she thought. Sure enough, as she entered the living room, Kasper was sprawled out on the couch in shorts and a vest, controller in hand and eyes glued to the action currently playing out on the TV screen.

"Yeah, we had a good time," she replied, kissing him on the head.

"Cool. Phoebe get home okay?" he asked, eyes still fixed on the TV.

"Yeah, I, um, I just dropped her off. You want a top up?" she asked, noticing the empty wine glass on the table by the sofa.

"Oh, yeah, cool. Thanks babe," he replied, finally taking his eyes away from his game to look at her. She picked up his glass and walked into the kitchen, taking a new bottle of wine from the refrigerator, and unscrewing the cap.

Why was he asking about Phoebe? said a voice somewhere in the back of her head.

Why does he *care if she got home safe or not?*

You know why, don't you?

"I do," she said to herself. "I do know why."

He's fucking her, or at least wants *to. And what do* you *want?*

"I want to kill them," she said out loud, though there was nobody else around to hear her. She put the wine and the glass down and opened the small cupboard under the sink. A moment or two of rummaging later, she emerged with exactly what she had been looking for: the rat poison. Although they had never actually had any issues with pests or vermin of any kind, she liked to keep traps and treatments handy just in case. She poured a liberal amount into his glass and topped it up with red wine, giving it a stir with a spoon for good measure.

This should work, she thought. *But just in case it doesn't…*

With the large glass of wine in her hand and the heavy marble rolling pin tucked into the back waistband of her leggings, she made her way back into the living room and handed him his drink.

"Ah, thanks babe," he said, accepting the glass and taking one deep gulp before turning his attention back to his game once more.

"I'm heading up," she said, and backed out of the living room before making her way upstairs. A few minutes later, having undressed, washed, brushed her teeth, and tied her hair back, she lay down in bed with the rolling pin safely hidden beneath her pillows. She had almost drifted off when she heard Kasper come up the stairs and head into the bathroom, barely closing the door in time before vomiting violently into the toilet.

Selina smiled.

It's working, she concluded.

A few minutes later, Kasper crawled into bed beside her and turned his bedside light on as he clambered in.

"Babe… I don't feel well," he said, and she turned to look at him in the light. Sure enough, he looked awful. His skin had taken on a sickly, pallid hue, and he was shaking violently. Blood had started to trickle from his nose and his breath had become raspy and inconsistent.

"I think I need to go to the hospital…" he said, sounding more like a child now than a man of nearly thirty.

"Okay, I'll call an ambulance," she said, sitting up and turning on her own bedside light. She reached down as if to pick up her mobile phone but instead withdrew the rolling pin from beneath her pillow and swung hard toward his face. The heavy marble tool struck him in the forehead with a satisfying *crack,* and blood no longer flowed from his nose alone. Selina did not stop at one blow but continued to beat Kasper on the head and around the face with the rolling pin, hitting him over and over, not stopping even when she knew he was long since dead.

The inevitable ache in her arm finally forced her to relent in her vicious attack and she dropped the pin down onto Kasper's viscera-soaked side of the bed. She looked for a long moment at her handiwork, taking in the spatter pattern on the wallpaper, the mass of pink and yellow pulp which had formerly been her partner's handsome face, and the blood which stained her own hands, arms, and nightwear. She smiled and leaned across the bed to turn off Kasper's light before turning off her own and curled up tight to sleep once more.

Selina slept soundly, her dreams pleasant and engrossing, and she did not stir until her alarm woke her up early the next morning. Kasper's blood and brain matter had now dried tight to her skin, so she decided to shower first and eat breakfast afterwards in a reversal of her usual routine. She threw back the covers with a yawn and a stretch and jumped out of bed with such gusto that she disturbed Kasper's cold, eviscerated body, and she watched with mild amusement as it tumbled off the bed and onto the floor with a sickening thud.

Making for the bathroom, Selina peeled off her blood-soaked nightwear and climbed into the shower, the hot water as pleasant and soothing as it was effective in removing the final traces of Kasper from her body. She closed her eyes; the steam which was quickly filling the room made it impossible to see anything in any case.

Well done, Selina. Well done. But there is one more to go. Two down, and one more to go... said the voice in the back of her mind.

"Yes," she said out loud, allowing some of the hot water to trickle into her mouth.

And you know who it has to be, don't you? it continued.

"Yes," she repeated.

Before long she was out of the shower, dry now and with her robe tied tight around her as she made her way into their dressing room to pick up Kasper's favourite leather belt. Downstairs she went next and flicked on the kettle. She had so far made no attempt to hide, clean, or otherwise disturb the grizzly scene on the floor above her.

She didn't have to.

She wasn't going to live much longer anyway.

Selina smiled as she continued to make her coffee, stopping for a moment only to decide whether she would prefer to eat toast or porridge oats before she hanged herself in the garage with her dead boyfriend's leather belt.

Porridge, she decided at length, and began to prepare her breakfast. She soon made her way into the living room where she curled up on the couch and switched on the TV, tuning into her preferred 24hr news station. Moving Kasper's empty wine glass onto the floor, she placed her hot coffee mug down on the side table as she listened absently to the news anchor report on the stories of the day, not really paying too much attention.

"...still have no leads in the tragic double homicide of Christian and Evelyn Nicholas who were found dead in their home on Christmas eve. A police spokesman has said…"

Selena turned off the TV and finished her breakfast and coffee in silence. After she had placed the used dishes into the sink a few minutes later, she picked up one of the stools which sat at the kitchen counter and made her way to the garage, Kasper's belt rolled up in her dressing gown pocket.

It did not take her long to identify the steel beam which ran the length of the garage that Kasper and his brother Jonas had built just last year. Selena tied the belt firmly around it and stood upon the stool, keeping her balance in check until all preparations had been made. Once she had secured the other end of the belt firmly against her throat and had given the belt a few exploratory tugs to ensure its integrity, she closed her eyes and slowed her breathing.

Good, Selina, good. You killed them, you killed them both. Now you must die, too. She had come to accept the voice in the back of her head, the same voice she had heard issuing from the mouth of her reflection in the Hall of Mirrors and agreed wholeheartedly with its verdict.

In one smooth movement she jumped into the air with both feet, aiming slightly ahead of herself and away from the safety of the stool. Within moments Selina was dead, hanging by her neck three feet from the ground.

"Hey, you listening? Come on, let's go get a hotdog," said Phoebe, staring in amusement at the blank expression on Selina's face. Her friend, who had complained about coming into the Hall of Mirrors in the first place, now stood transfixed by her own wonky reflection.

"Huh? Oh, yeah, sorry. I must have zoned out there for a second," replied Selina, shaking her head to clear the cobwebs in her mind.

"Come on, I'm starving," said Phoebe, taking Selina by the arm and leading her out of the attraction.

Neither girl looked back as they departed, so neither saw that Selina's reflection had remained in place after they had left.

Mirror-Selina continued to stare out from its own side of the divide, grinning, laughing quietly to itself as it watched the two friends leave.

Well done, Selina.

"What do you think Kasper and JJ are doing right now?" asked Phoebe.

"Oh, you know our boys, probably playing video games and drinking red wine," replied Selina. Both girls laughed and continued to walk toward the enticing smell of the hotdog stand.

Selina's eyes narrowed and she threw a sidelong look at her friend.

*Why's she asking about Kasper? s*aid a familiar voice in the back of her mind…

SUPER MAX

She'd told him a thousand times, drilled it into him until she was blue in the face:

"Look both ways before you cross the road, Max."

*

Max had always been an excitable kid, prone to fits of laughter and running around the garden for no apparent reason. The slightest sign of something even remotely interesting had always rendered him awestruck.

His eighth birthday had been hectic to say the least.

Max's parents - Aidan and Clara Wheeler - had showered him with brightly wrapped presents and allowed him to eat as much birthday cake as he wanted, despite knowing all too well that he would be sick afterwards. Of Max's gifts, quite aside from the action figures, video games, colouring books, and science sets he had received, it was the bright yellow football to which he had taken a particular liking.

Kicking it around the garden and chasing down his own passes, he was in his element, ignorant to the fact that all this running would only serve to speed up the inevitable cake-induced sickness. Aidan and Clara let him play, happy for him to burn off as much energy as possible while they tidied up indoors and treated themselves to an early afternoon glass of wine; they had earned it today.

So happy was Max with his new football that his enthusiasm inevitably got the better of him and the ball ended up going over the garden gate and out towards the street.

"I'll get it!" Max shouted. Without missing a step, he made his way out of the back-garden gate, following the trajectory of his bouncing ball out onto the main street in front of the house. Upon hearing their son shout out to them, Max's parents turned to peer through the glass double doors into the back garden.

A garden now devoid of their child.

Panicked, they ran to the living room window which looked out onto the main road. Standing out brightly against the afternoon clouds and dark road beyond, Aidan and Clara could only look on in horror while, as if in slow motion, their son's bright yellow football bounced inexorably toward the tarmac, followed closely by a grinning Max.

He was focused solely on retrieving his prized ball and did not hear his parents' screams from inside the house, nor did he register the enormous, blue Freightliner semi-truck roaring toward him until it was mere inches away.

Max was only cognizant of the danger at the very last second, so did not have time for conscious thought. Instead, his instincts took over and he squeezed his eyes shut, throwing out a hand as if to ward off the incoming truck.

And stopped it dead in its tracks.

Max could not quite believe what he saw as he slowly opened his eyes. The truck, the monstrous machine which had hurtled toward him at such great velocity, stood motionless at the tips of his fingers, its cab crumpled and smoking in an arc around his still-outstretched hand. Slowly bringing the hand away from the truck and up toward his eyes, Max stared in disbelief as he beheld neither a scratch nor a bruise to speak of, despite the damage he had caused to the semi.

The driver, Max suddenly thought, and ran around to the side of the cab to check on its occupant. Max was only a kid, and the handle to the cab door was well out of reach, way above his head. Still, he had to help, he couldn't just leave the driver to his fate. He bent his knees and leapt into the air, aiming to reach the handle and all too aware that he couldn't possibly jump that high.

But he did.

Max's jump took him up past the door and onto the roof of the cab itself.

Whoa... he thought, and he realised that something strange was happening to him. *No time to think about that now*, he resolved, his eyes darting to-and-fro, searching for a way to help the stricken truck driver. He spotted a tear in the metal roof caused by the impact and thrust his hand inside and pulled. With no more effort than opening a can of soda, Max peeled back the roof and lifted the driver out and threw him over his comically small shoulders. Max jumped down from the cab roof and made his way to his front lawn to lay the driver down on the soft grass.

Mom and Dad will know what to do, he thought, stepping away from the driver and looking back at the truck. The smell of smoke and fuel filled the air and, as if Max's mere gaze was the cue it had been waiting for, the truck burst into flames with a *whoosh*.

Max cast a glance over his shoulder to confirm to himself that the driver was indeed okay, then stepped toward the flaming truck. Though he could feel the heat of the roaring flames, he felt no pain from it and was certain that he would not were he to thrust his hand inside the inferno.

Something had happened to Max, something had changed.

He looked up into the sky, then back down at his hands, turning them over and taking in every inch, still in shock at his own actions. He needed some space; he needed to think. Aware now that his parents were coming out of the house and running toward him, Max bent his knees and summoned all the strength he could muster. He leapt, bursting into the air at supersonic speed, and continued his ascent until he was high amongst the clouds. Eventually he slowed his climb and stopped in place, floating thousands of feet above the ground.

I can fly, too, he realised.

He had to get away, he had to find somewhere quiet to think, so he chose a direction at random, levelled himself out horizontally and took off at great speed. Before too long he could make out the city below and made his way down, descending slowly toward the colossal grey structures. He selected the tallest building he could find and landed with a thump on its roof. The view of the city from this hitherto inaccessible vantage point threatened to take his very breath away.

There he sat for a while, thinking, really *thinking,* trying to make sense of what was happening to him. The best his young mind could come up with was that he had been born this way, and the fear and panic he had felt in that split second before the truck hit must have activated something within him which had lain dormant until that traumatic event. The truth was that he didn't know, maybe he would never know, but one thing that he *did* know was that he was going to use this gift.

I can help people, he thought. *I can be a hero, like Lightspeed or the Midnight Man.*

He could not go home, that much he also knew. He was confident that his parents had seen his wondrous feats, so they knew he was safe. He had to plan now. The first thing he needed was a disguise; if he was going to be a hero, he couldn't just walk around in his cargo pants and dinosaur t-shirt now, could he? At very least he needed a mask. But how was he going to do it? How could he possibly make himself a hero costume? He didn't even have any mon- *Wait,* Max thought, and he thrust his hand into his pocket excitedly. Registering the crisp feel of paper against his skin, he pulled out the $30 his Aunt Shelley had sent him for his birthday.

Yes! Now I can get a costume.

Max was all too aware that he was now in a huge, bustling city, so finding what he needed shouldn't be a problem. Very soon he emerged from the *Phoenix Fancy Dress and Joke Shop* and ran down the nearest alleyway before once again hurtling himself up and into the air, making sure he kept a tight hold on the bag which contained his new costume. He landed on the same roof he had found earlier and made short work of ripping open the packaging and changing into his costume.

Not just a new outfit, but a new identity, a new purpose, a new Max.

A Super Max.

He was now dressed head to foot in black and green, with a long flowing black cape billowing behind him in the wind, and a green domino mask covering his eyes and cheeks. Max hid his regular clothes behind a rooftop ventilation outlet and walked to the edge of the building. He stood for a few moments and breathed deeply as he beheld the city below as the sunlight began to fade.

Super Max, he thought, and he jumped off the roof and into the air once more, his characteristic smile on full display for the citizens below.

When the sun goes away, the criminals come out. Max had read enough comic books to know *that* for sure. This city was no different, and it wasn't long before he heard a cry for help from somewhere north of his position.

Super hearing too, huh? Cool.

Max followed the sound to its source and he soon found himself in a parking lot on the outskirts of the city. It was a quiet spot, neither well known nor frequently used; the perfect place for a mugging, as it turned out. The cries, he realised, were coming from a girl who could not have been a day over nineteen, struggling with two men attempting to steal her purse at knifepoint. Her pleas had fallen on deaf ears thus far, and Max knew it was up to him now. He was the only one who could save the girl.

"Let her go," Max boomed from behind the two men who instantly turned around, more than ready for a fight.

The two would-be muggers stood still and silent for a moment, confused and shocked by the appearance of the girl's saviour: a young boy barely four feet tall and dressed head to foot in a green and black super-hero costume. The moment soon passed and both men threw back their heads in fits of riotous laughter, the girl's arm still clutched tightly in one of the duo's large hands.

"Isn't it past your bedtime? Get the fuck out of here, kid."

"I said let her go, I don't want to hurt you," Max replied, unmoving. The novelty had worn off and the thugs weren't laughing any more.

"Last chance, kid. Get the fuck out of here or we'll do you like we're gonna do her."

Max sighed for dramatic effect. "I warned you…" he said, springing to action. He flew at the thug who still grasped the struggling girl, and not only opened up the man's hands to free the captive girl but continued to bend back his fingers until they broke with a satisfying *crunch*. The man fell to his knees, his broken hand tucked under the opposite arm, but Max lifted him by his coat collar and casually threw him aside to land skidding some twenty feet away.

The second man had watched the whole scene play out in front of him with a mix of bewilderment and terror on his face. He froze in place as Max, turning away from his defeated foe, fixed him with an unblinking stare.

Then it happened.

Max's green eyes narrowed in a frown, his irises adopting a new, redder hue, as droplets of blood permeating an emerald lake. Glowing now and starting to hiss, Max's eyes burned like once-colossal stars now crushed under the weight of their own gravity. The thug, his instincts having taken over his conscious intentions, promptly pissed himself on the spot and was vaporised a moment later as beams of pure, burning hot energy burst from Max's eyes and obliterated the criminal where he stood. Max turned to the girl, who also stood staring in horror and awe, and nodded sharply, with the dying embers of the furious red energy still dancing in his eyes.

"It's okay, you're safe now," he said, before turning his gaze skywards and bending his knees. Max propelled himself into the air once more, and for a time he circled the city, his eyes darting here and there, his ears keen and his senses alert for any sign of trouble or danger. He eventually decided there was none, at least not at the moment, and he soon found himself back on the highest roof in the city once more. He retrieved the hidden bag containing his regular clothes and changed back into them. He sat perched on the roof for what seemed like an eternity to a boy of his age. The skies were dark, and the air was turning bitterly cold, especially at this height.

Max, however, did not shiver, he dismissed the evening chills as surely as he had shrugged off the heat of the burning truck.

I did it, he thought. *I saved her. I* am *a hero. I can't explain what happened, but that's okay, I don't have to explain it. I just need to use these powers for good, to help people like I helped that girl. I'll start with this city and I'll check in on my parents from time to time, but I can't go home. This is what I do now. No - this is who I* am *now.*

A hero.

Max held his hand out in front of him, the hand that had stopped the truck, the hand that had started *all* of this, and made a fist.

***

"He squeezed my hand! Doctor? Doctor! He just squeezed my hand!" exclaimed Clara as she sat beside Max's bed, staring through tear-soaked eyes at the multitude of tubes, monitors, and sensors which were currently the only things keeping her son alive. The mechanical *whirring* of the ventilator and the electronic *beeps* from the monitors had been the only real sounds which had rung out in Max's room for days, so the register of Clara's strained voice sent the doctor and nurses running into the boy's room immediately. The doctor scrutinised the readouts and checked Max meticulously, then nodded to herself in silent confirmation of her suspicions. She turned to lay a gentle hand on Clara's shoulder while she knelt down to lock eyes with both of the boy's parents.

"It's normal for muscles to spasm and contract in situations like this. The brain can sometimes show some small signs of activity and the body maintains some of its most basic functions when it's in, well, when a patient is as poorly as Max. We also believe that coma patients can sometimes experience vivid hallucinations, but I urge you, Mr. and Mrs. Wheeler, please do not get your hopes up. Max is still a very, very sick young man."

The doctor was right, they knew. The truck had hit Max *hard*, and it was a miracle he had survived at all, let alone for this long.

He was a fighter, they knew this, but while they trusted the doctors and the nursing team implicitly and completely, they also knew deep down that Max may never wake up.

Clara still held her son's hand as she lowered her head and wept anew, and the doctor slowly walked away, leaving Max's parents alone with their son once more. When the tidal wave of sorrow and pain had finally passed, and Clara had regained some semblance of control over her broken heart and shattered nerves, her blurry eyes fell upon the burst and dirty yellow football on the floor beside Max's hospital bed.

THE NEW GUY

Hey, over here. Hey, you....
Yes, YOU.
Jesus, come on man, get your fucking head in the game.
Come here, there's a good boy. Do that again and you might even get a biscuit.
Not much of a talker, huh? Well, that's okay; makes my job a whole lot fucking easier.
Your first day, huh? Well, we've got a lot to do, so grab, your shit, follow me, don't touch anything, and maybe try shutting up for a change.
No? Nothing? Fuck; tough crowd. Well, it's early so I'll let it slide, plus is stinks worse than my fucking grandma down there, and she's been dead for ten years.
Right, okay. Got your hard hat on? Got your flashlight?
Okay.
Clip this thing onto your belt like this, and – no, wait, here. Like, yeah, that's it.
See? Learning already.
Okay, give it a quick yank - and I don't mean your fucking pecker – and, yeah, that's plenty tight.
Alright, follow me down, watch your footing, and if you think you can smell, piss, shit, and homeless fucking bums, don't worry, that'll just be the piss, shit, and homeless fucking bums.

Right, come on…

*

Right, so what we're doing today is clearing out the fat-bergs and the shit-bergs.

Really? How the fuck did you get this job if you don't…

Basically, all the shit, oil, cooking fat, food, fucking tampons and whatever the fuck else people flush or swill away into the sewers tends to, sort of, clump together every once in a while and it can block the flow of water and fucking back up the network.

Yeah, it is *bad; toxic-waste-spilling-out-onto-the-streets bad.*

So we go down with all this hi-tech stuff and blast or poke it loose so the little fucking kiddies topside aren't playing around in fucking sludge.

Me? Oh, about seven years now, give or take.

Yeah, I do enjoy it, funnily enough. You get used to the smell, and at least down here, whether you're by yourself or double-crewed, you don't have to deal with other people's shit – well, no, I mean we do literally *have to deal with other people's shit, but you know what I mean.*

Gives you time to think, you know?

Okay, come on… Shit-berg, twelve o'clock.

*

Yeah, that one's a fucking doozy. We're probably downstream of some obese, kebab-eating motherfucker with about a year left on his ticket. Urgh… That's a big one alright.

You? Well, you hand me that hose and go stand by the controls; I'll do this one, then you can go do the next. We'll alternate as we go along, deal?

Haha! "Deal"- As if this is a negotiation; you'll do as you're fucking told, New Guy.

Right, when I say so, gimme about 30% power to start off with, and try not to fucking kill yourself, okay?

This isn't a fucking garden hose; enough power and the water will cut your fucking arm off; I'm serious.

Right… Just lemme… Almost…

Okay, time to bust this bitch: Now!

Right! There we go. Pretty cool, eh? It's good when they just fucking crack open and crumble like that; this thing here really does a number on them.

Cool, so that's that, on to the next one. Wind that shit up and follow me. And watch your step, we're going pretty deep and there's no telling what we could trip over or stumble across.

*

What? Yeah, I heard about that.

Three? No, no, no… I think it's more like five. Don't worry though, the papers got it wrong; they didn't work for us – well – one of them might have, maybe, I can't be sure.

It just goes to show, though – and let this be one of those fucking "teachable moments" – that it's dangerous work we do down here. Between the dark, the shit, the potential to fucking slice your own neck open if you piss about with that machine… Not to mention the clowns and monsters that live down here.

Haha! I'm just fucking with you.

The only clown down here is you, you fucking prick, haha.

No, it is dangerous, and those five or six guys they either pulled out from down here in pieces, or the poor fuckers they never actually found are proof enough of that.

Okay, come on…

*

What? You'll have to speak up, man, it somehow gets louder the deeper we get.

WHAT?

Okay! No need to fucking shout…

There should be a ladder in about two, maybe three hundred yards that'll take us down to the next level. It gets very dark and very dangerous down there, so just listen to me and do whatever the fuck I tell you, okay?

No, I need to hear you say it. Say "I'm happy to come along, and I will do whatever the fuck I'm told".

What are you grinning for? I'm deadly fucking serious.

Say it, or I drag your ass to the surface right now and you can fuck off back to the unemployment queue.

Go on…

There's a good boy.

Now come the fuck on, and watch your step.

Ah, there it is. Right, I'll go first. Then you lower all that shit down to me, and follow once I've secured it, okay?

Right, here goes.

And maybe try to breathe through your mouth; it smells like death down here.

*

Fuck me, that shit's heavy.

Okay, the kit is secure; come on down.

Cool, cool. You all set? Right.

Okay, so we're gonna leave all this heavy shit here and collect it on our way back up.

Why? Because we don't fucking need it, that's why. It's small-tools work from her on out. That should suit you and your tiny tool just right, eh? Haha! I'm just fucking with you. Come on; it's a bit of a trek, but it'll be worth it once we get to where we're going.

Jesus, enough with all the fucking questions! I thought you were supposed to be observing and doing as you were fucking told? Yeah, that's what I thought.

Come on and watch your step; there's no telling what you might step in once you get this deep underground.

Ah! Here we are!

You see? The door? Well, you might not be able to see the door itself in this darkness, but you see the light coming out from under and around it? Yeah, that!

What?

Well of course there's someone in there; why else would there be a light on?

Fucking idiot...

Prank? Yeah, sure. Exactly.

It's a "New Guy, Day One" kind of thing.

You got me. Just a joke.

Prank...

Joke...

Practical...

Hazing...

Joke...

Practical.... Prank.

Now get the fuck inside before I cut your fucking throat.

*

Why so scared, sweetheart?

What, this? Yeah, of course it's real. I could hardly cut your throat with a fake knife, now could I?

What's in there? Well; you're about to find out.

Now get moving. One foot in front of the other, there's a good boy.

Now open the door.

OPEN – THE – DOOR.

I'm not fucking kidding; open it right now or you'll be dead before you hit the floor.

That's it… Pull, man. Harder! It's been a little while since it was opened from this side.

What sounds?

Screaming?

Oh, yeah, of course; I don't even hear it anymore. Funny, isn't it? It's a bit like the smell down here; you get used to it.

Piss, shit, nappies tampons, dogs, cats, men-women-children, pleading, screaming… It's all just ambience.

Now I know you heard me tell you to open that fucking door, and you promised to exactly what you were told.

There's a good little boy.

*

On your knees! Right now!

Bow, you insolent fuck! Like this, see?

Do you have any idea whose presence you are in?
Haha! I see you have added to the overall levels of piss and shit down here; I hope you weren't planning on re-wearing those pants. Well, not that its gonna matter much anymore.

Master! Oh, divine Lord of Chaos; Ruler of the Deep; Bringer of Light; Scourge of Eons; Key to Transcendence; Seer of All – I have brought unto you a willing sacrifice, that you may – if it be in your great design – confer upon me The Sight!

That means you, you dumb fuck, get up. On your feet, now. Take off those clothes. Do as I command, infidel! Unbeliever! You dare stand in the almighty presence of an eternal, ancient, all-powerful being like Roloth the Defiler, and you would question your place?

What? Me? I'm your Team Leader, you prick.
My name?
Oh... Well...
I don't actually remember my name; it's been years since I've heard it, centuries even. Nobody has spoken the name my filthy infidel mother gave me since the old days; the days before the fucking internet and phones, before cars and planes, before science killed the Christian God...
No, don't worry about my name.
You can just call me High Priest.

What? Are you serious? Who's gonna come looking for you, exactly?

The Police? Yeah, right. Who's gonna call them?

Head Office, he says! Haha!

Oh, you poor fool, grasping at straws. Have you ever actually been to head office? Of course not. Not that it's any of your concern anymore, but we don't actually go to head office; we just get our assignments and crack on.

One of the reasons we chose this filthy, stinking work as the best possible cover to serve our great and glorious master Roloth.

Yeah, "we" – what, you don't think I'm alone, surely? How do you think you got this job in the first place?

Yes, now he understands… we have a very meticulous recruitment process.

It's funny, actually, 'cause this is all kind of your own fault, really. No, really; you'd be amazed at the kind of irrelevant, personal shit people put on their CVs these days. "Single, no dependants, willing to relocate".

You fucking idiot…You see what you've done there? You've folded yourself up real tight, crawled up inside a piss-soaked envelope, licked your-fucking-self, and posted yourself right to His feet.

No; nobody is going to miss you… *You said so yourself in black and fucking white.*

In fact, come to think of it, nobody but me has even seen your face. Well, me and Him.

No, don't cover your eyes! Look at Him! Look into his Light!
Be not afraid; glory awaits us all on the other side!
Time, light, whole Universes exist within his glory! You need only submit to his will and offer yourself unto his eternal greatness!
He was here before life first twitched its way into agonising existence on this putrid Earth, and he will be here long after the Sun has cast off its heat and devoured this insignificant solar system.
So transcend; be free of the pain and suffering which masquerades as "free-will", as life itself.
Transcend.
Look at Him; stand unblinking before His mighty light!

And try not to scream.
This will hurt.

LYDIA

"I don't know you." she said suddenly from directly behind him. Connor nearly jumped out of his skin; he hadn't even known she was there.

*

It was another glorious day in Topeka, Kansas. The temperature was easily in the 90s despite it not yet being noon. Birds sang their songs, cars meandered by as if in slow motion; the summer day capturing them in its gravity-well and slowing them to a leisurely crawl.

The neighbourhood in which Connor lived with his mom was a quiet, sleepy suburb. Houses lined both sides of a well-maintained road, and a car sat in front of every second house, more or less.

His mother was at work, and although Connor wasn't sure what her job was exactly, he knew it had something to do with magazines. Connor was spending his first summer truly by himself; now that he was eleven, he no longer required full-time supervision.

As she had fussed over him that very morning, ensuring he had finished his breakfast, taken a shower, and brushed his teeth, she had reminded him *again* of the words which she had drilled into his head daily since his school closed for the summer.

"Your lunch is in the blue box in the refrigerator - just take it out, put it onto a plate, and set the microwave for three minutes."

"Yes Mom." he had sighed.

"You can grab a snack later, but just *one*, Connor, just one."

"*Yes* Mom." puffing out his breath.

"And remember," his mom, Lizzy, had continued "…if you need anything, if there's an emergency or you hurt yourself or *anything* what do you do?"

"I go across the street to Mr and Mrs Kingsley's and they will call you if they need to - I know what to do, Mom."

And he did; Connor Harris was a good kid. As an only-child raised single-handedly by his mother since his Dad walked out when Connor was still just a baby, he pretty much kept to himself. He loved nothing more than sitting in his room playing video games or reading those Super Hero comics he was so enamoured of - *The Green Arrow* and *Batman* being his absolute favourites. Connor had never really gotten into any real trouble at school, had kept up decent if not Earth-shattering grades, and had a small group of loyal, similarly quiet friends. In fact, the only time he ever really went outside was to kick his soccer ball around. Eschewing the more traditional pursuits of baseball, basketball, or the NFL, European-style soccer was Connor's only real sporting interest.

It was with that very same ball which Connor had been playing, outside in the late morning sunshine, when the voice had startled him out of his daydream of scoring the winning goal in a cup final, and he spun around to face the owner of this sudden exclamation.

Easily a year younger and a foot shorter, blonde hair in pigtails and blue pinafore dress immaculately pressed and clean, she stood staring at him as if waiting for him to answer a question he couldn't remember being asked.

"Um, what?" he said after regaining his composure.

"I said I don't know you." the girl replied.

"I'm Connor, Connor Harris. I live over there," he replied, pointing behind him toward his house.

She leaned her body ever so slightly to peer around him, following the direction of his extended finger to look at his house almost as if to verify his story.

"You gave me a fright; I didn't even hear you come up behind me." he said.

"I'm sorry about that." was all she offered in reply.

"Who are you, anyway; I don't think I know you either, but we haven't been here that long. About two years now is all." Connor said, finally finding his voice following his sharp shock moments earlier.

"I'm Lydia," she replied. "I live around the corner from here."

"I've never seen you at school," Connor said, frowning.

"Oh, I don't go to school. My momma teaches me at home; she doesn't like it when I go outside and doesn't really like me playing with other kids," Lydia confided.

"Oh, that sucks, huh? Why does she do that?" Connor genuinely wanted to know. Lydia hesitated; an unnamed concern taking shape in the furrow of her brow and the purse of her lips.

"I'd better go. My momma. I'd better go." she said and turned on her heel to leave Connor alone once more.

The blaring *BEEEEP* of a car horn caused Connor to turn away from Lydia as a mean-looking red pickup truck - old Mr Gallagher's, he was pretty sure - alerted him to the fact that his soccer ball had rolled into the road while he had been speaking to Lydia.

He held his hands in the air, palms outward in a placatory gesture, and waited until Mr Gallagher's truck had cleared the road and ran to retrieve his ball. By the time he turned back around to the general direction in which Lydia had exited, she was gone; gone as silently as she had appeared.

"Just like Batman" he said out loud to nobody in particular.

Once he was back indoors and was lying comfortably on his bed, Connor was surrounded by posters of his heroes. Soccer stars and Super Heroes stared back at him while he lay, game controller in hand. He was engrossed in a game when his concentration was momentarily broken by the rumble in his tummy and subsequent glance at the clock on his bedroom wall.

4pm, Good, he thought. His mom would be home soon. He'd long since warmed and up and eaten the lunch from the blue box in the refrigerator - Lasagne, he was pleased to discover - and had taken his one allocated snack, a fun-sized Snickers bar which really *was* fun, he had reflected upon its consumption. But that was a few hours ago, and he was now hungry as hell - scoring winning goals in imaginary cup finals really works up an appetite.

His head was now firmly back in his game, and he hardly noticed the next hour go by until he heard the tell-tale crunch of tires on gravel, and heard his mother enter the house shouting his name to check he was indeed inside.

"Connor, honey?"

"Up here Mom. How was your day?" He *was* a good kid.

"Ah, same as usual…" she replied, already coming up the stairs.

"Gimme fifteen and I'll bore you with all the details over dinner."

She stopped off in his room to briefly kiss him on the head, then headed straight for the bathroom to shower away the working day. Within the hour, Lizzy and Connor Harris were sat at the table and very much ready to devour the enormous spaghetti bolognese they had made together; cooking was just starting to make Connor's 'list' alongside soccer, video games, and comics.

With the table set and the piping-hot food served, they sat down and tucked in with neither preamble nor prayer. They were not a religious household, a fact with which certain of Lizzy's relatives were none-too-pleased. Lizzy took a long, slow sip of her red wine and looked affectionately at her son across the table.

"You know I hate leaving you alone, right?" she asked.

He held up a finger while he chewed and swallowing a long piece of spaghetti, then looked his mother in the eye and answered her question.

"Yeah, I know. But it can't be helped. I honestly don't mind," He threw her a lop-sided smile and continued "You know I'm happy to sit and read comics all day, Mom." She smiled back at him earnestly, more proud of him each day.

"I know, sweetheart. I know you have your comics and your video games, but I just wish you weren't, you know." She let the unspoken word hang between them like a light bulb suspended on a wire above the table.

"Alone?" he offered. His mother nodded her response and busied herself with her meal. They were content to simply eat and drink for another couple of minutes before his mother offered up a new topic of conversation.

"Hey, I forgot to tell you. You remember Josephine, my friend from work?" Seeing the confusion on Connor's face, she elaborated.

"You remember? Short? Dark hair?"

"*A couple of sandwiches overweight?*" she added, whispering conspiratorially.

"She came to our house-warming with her husband and her son, Tommy."

"Oh yeah, I remember," said Connor, the penny having dropped. "Tommy had red hair."

"Yeah, well she told me that Tommy was feeling a little lonely too these last couple of days. All his friends have gone off home for the summer, you know?"

Connor nodded for her to continue.

"Well, I just thought; why don't I invite them over some time, huh? I can sit and chat to Josephine and you and Tommy can play together. Doesn't that sound fun?"

Seeing that his mom was positively beaming at this idea, he did the right thing and agreed despite it sounding like a *horribl*e idea to him. "Sure Mom, that sound great. But, hey, speaking of being lonely, I have some news too."

Lizzy tilted her head ever so slightly to the left, betraying her intrigue "Yeah?"

"Yeah; I made a new friend today."

"Oh! That's great honey!" his mother replied in genuine pleasure with a dash of amazement thrown into the emotional cocktail. "What's his name?"

"*Her* name is Lydia. I've never seen her before today, but I know we haven't been here that long, so…"

"Lydia, huh? Does she go to your school?"

"No," Connor replied. "She said her mom, 'Momma' she calls her, home-schools her and doesn't like her playing with other kids."

Lizzy's eyebrows came together in a frown "Home-schooled? And not allowed to play with other kids? Is she, I mean, does she have… Did she look, you know…. *normal*?"

"Yeah, she looked perfectly normal to me. You know, for a *girl*…" Connor's cheeks and neck had started to blush.

"She said she lives just around the corner at the bottom of the street, here," he said, pointing outside, "but she took off suddenly and I didn't see which way she went"

"Huh." his mother mused.

"Lydia, huh? Huh."

The following morning progressed in much the same manner as the previous, with Connor up, dressed, and eating breakfast while his mother darted to and fro getting ready for work. She fretted, tying up her hair, grabbing her bag, making sure she had something packed up for lunch - the usual hullabaloo of a workday morning.

She left him the same instructions once again - lunch is in the refrigerator, he's allowed one snack, if anything goes wrong he's to go straight to the Kingsley's - and he rolled his eyes in exaggerated exasperation as she rattled of her check list.

"I know, Mom. I'll be fine. Have a good day at work," he said smiling.

She smiled back, kissed him on the head, and shouted "Love you!" as she left through the front door and made her way to work. A quiet calm settled over the house now that his mom had left, and Connor casually finished his breakfast, put the used dishes in the dishwasher and sat in front of the TV for a while, though he wasn't really paying much attention to what was actually on. His eyes started to wander, heavy with early morning lethargy. His gaze drifted away from the TV to the clock on the wall, then to the couch to his right, further round the room toward the main living room window…

"Aaargh!" he exclaimed in shock, almost jumping out of his skin. There, standing outside and staring at him through the window, was Lydia.

Once she was sure he had seen her - it was pretty obvious from his reaction - she smiled and motioned for him to join her outside. He slipped on his sneakers and exited the house through the same door his mother had left through a little earlier. He stepped outside and noted the heat immediately. The sun was once again baking hot, even now at around 9:30am, and it would only get hotter as the day wore on.

"Jesus, you scared the life out of me! What were you doing standing at my window!?" Connor spat out.

"I was waiting for you to see me." Lydia replied deadpan, the concept of rhetorical questions seemingly lost on her. Connor blew out a long, composing breath and immediately felt calmer.

"So, what are you up to? You playing in the street?" he asked.

"No, I just wanted to come and see you. My momma doesn't like me playing with other kids, but she doesn't know about you."

"Cool," was the only thing Connor could think to say in reply, and Lydia's face suddenly broke into a full, beaming smile.

"So what do you want to play?" she asked earnestly.

"Uh, I don't know…. Do you like soccer?" Connor suggested.

"I've never played soccer. My momma doesn't like me playing with other kids." replied Lydia.

"Uh, okay, well, here…" said Connor, picking up the ball from where it lay on the Harris' front lawn.

"You stand between the gate posts, and I'll try to kick the ball past you. You have to stop it, you're the Goalie, see?"

"Okay!" Lydia beamed.

They each took up their respective positions and Connor took his first shot at goal, keeping it tame to give Lydia a chance. Or so he thought as he watched her outstretched hand completely miss the ball, and into the *net* it went.

"Awww drat," Lydia exclaimed, though seemingly not the slightest bit discouraged. Connor retrieved the ball and lined up another shot; this one too flew straight into the top corner - Lydia truly *had* never played soccer before.

"I don't like this game," she said, immediately deflated following Connor's second goal.

"It's okay, I'll take a few more shots and then we can swap; I'll be the Goalie and you can score." he said, explaining how the game proceeds.

"I SAID I DON'T LIKE THIS GAME!" screamed Lydia, and a darkness seemed to fall over her face for a second like a widow at a funeral, veiled in black. Taken aback, Connor stood and tried to process this sudden outburst; he knew girls could be stroppy, but sheesh, this was a full-on tantrum.

"Okay, that's cool; what do you want to play next?" he said after a moment.

Lydia, the dark veil now lifted (Connor's imagination running wild... *damn comic books*), looked down at the floor for a moment then beamed up at him once again.

"Do you have any chalk?" she asked, as excited as a kid on Christmas morning.

"Um, yeah, sure... I'll go get some. Gimme a minute."

Connor went back inside the house, still a little confused by the Lydia's sudden angry outburst and went to his stationary supplies to retrieve a pack of coloured chalks. Returning outside, Lydia immediately took over proceedings.

"Yay! Right, okay, so you have to draw squares on the floor, like this..."

She explained the basics of a hopscotch grid to Connor and had him draw it out and number the boxes one to eight. She was delighted with the result and immediately went to the first square, proceeding to jump and land at intervals upon the numbered squares, gleefully reciting a rhyme as she went.

"One, two, three, four,
Place a lock upon my door.
Five, six, seven, eight,
Open up when it gets late.
Eight, seven, six, five,
Keep a secret: stay alive.
Four, three, two, one,
Don't make Daddy fetch his gun."

She landed on square one once more, a beaming smile on her face once again - *this* game she liked.

"One, two, three, four, place a lock upon my door..." she stopped suddenly and turned to face Connor.

"What time is it?" she asked, eyes wide. Connor wasn't wearing a watch and had left his phone inside.

"I don't know... ten? Ten thirty?"

Lydia's eyes were staring to fill with tears.

"Could you please check for me? I need to know what time it is. Momma doesn't like me playing with other kids."

"Sure, no problem, just wait here." Connor replied. He went inside and picked his phone up from the couch, touching its screen to bring it to life. The large, bright display showed it was 10.24am.

Not a bad guess, he thought. He headed back outside to tell Lydia the time and gloat about how close his guess had been, but she was nowhere to be seen. Connor surmised that she must not have wanted to wait for the answer and had instead just headed straight home. He shrugged his shoulders and decided it was too damn hot to play soccer outside right now anyway, so he simply went back inside and up to his room.

As he lay there on his bed, arms folded behind his head for comfort, he just couldn't shake that rhyme from his head.

"One, two, three, four,
Place a lock upon my door.
Five, six, seven, eight,
Open up when it gets late.
Eight, seven, six, five,
Keep a secret: stay alive.
Four, three, two, one,
Don't make Daddy fetch his gun."

He woke suddenly, just before 2pm; he'd nodded off and napped soundly following the morning's games with Lydia. His stomach was rumbling in protest, so Connor jumped up off the bed and headed downstairs to warm up his lunch. Twenty minutes later, once his hunger had been sated and the dishwasher stocked, he was at a bit of a loose end.

He replayed the morning's experiences with Lydia in his mind and was struck by how *strange* the girl was. The tantrum, the look in her eyes, and the sudden change in her voice all contrasted starkly with the sheer glee with which she proceeded down the hopscotch grid moments later. And then there were the tears, genuine tears born of fear and worry. Tears which interrupted her recital of that rhyme.

So weird, he thought.

Connor made the conscious decision to put the incident to one side and retired to his room once more to kill the next few hours in the company of his video games until his mother returned home from work.

Later, home slightly later than usual, his mother was in a poor humour, seemingly flustered by something unspoken and devoid of her usual disarming smile. She kicked off her shoes and headed immediately to the kitchen where she greeted her son and continued prepared their dinner still wearing her work clothes.

"Is everything okay, Mom?" Connor asked with a sincerity which belied his age. Lizzy paused in her food preparation and looked at him earnestly.

"Yes, honey. I'm sorry. It's just been a rough old day is all."

She pinched his cheek and threw him a wink, then continued with the dinner. They were soon sat at the table enjoying a huge and much needed roast.

"So…" said Connor, trying to prompt his mother into conversation.

"Hmm? Oh, yeah, well…" she started. "You know how I'm the editor in chief at the magazine?" He didn't, but he nodded anyway. "... well one of the guys - Jeremy - brought me a piece today about a serial killer over in England. Apparently, he killed a bunch of people and was driving round in an ice cream truck wearing their faces like masks…. It's *sick."*

Connor nodded along, fascinated and repulsed in equal measure.

"Well it's just not the kind of thing we publish. We're more celebrity gossip, fashion trends, skin-care tips, that sort of thing, you know?"

"So anyway, there was an argument, things got a little heated, and I had to pull rank on him so it's been a stressful day. How about you, anything to report?"

Anything to report, indeed, Connor thought.

"No, not really. It was hot so I went out to play soccer and ran into Lydia again. It was too hot though so I came inside and took a nap."

"Lydia again, huh?" his mother asked with an amused glint in her eye.

"So what's she like now you know her a bit better?"

"Honestly? She's a bit weird. I don't think we're gonna be friends" Connor replied before tucking back into his meal.

The rest of the evening came and went; Connor and his mother settling down to watch some trashy TV before saying goodnight and retiring to bed to each put their respective rough days behind them.

We're not gonna be friends, he repeated to himself when he was safely tucked up in his bed, making sure to fully cover his feet and ankles with the covers as a symbolic defence against the creeping, mounting fear which had been steadily growing him since morning.

Connor awoke the next morning feeling refreshed but a little frustrated. There was a frown on his brow and a shortness to his temper. He couldn't remember if he had dreamed last night, but knew that if he had they can't have been good dreams. He got up and went downstairs to breakfast, watching his mother get herself ready for work and listening to her remind him once again of his check-list for the day. His frustration suddenly began to take on a more identifiable, more tangible shape.

This routine is tiresome he thought; he was becoming bored, and - if he was truly honest with himself - a little resentful of his situation. He assured his mother that he knew where his food was, he knew where to go if anything happened, and that he was very much aware of his snack allocation, then watched her leave for work. Upon hearing the car pull out of the drive, Connor resolved to try something a little different today and just went straight back to his room.

He didn't want to listen to music or play video games, he just wanted to sleep. And sleep he did for an hour or so until an eerily musical "Co-nnooorrr," snapped him out of his slumber and brought the world back into bright, hot focus.

In order to discover the source of the voice - though he already knew to whom it belonged - he strode across to his bedroom window, peered out, and saw Lydia once again standing outside of his house.

She smiled up at him, motioning with her hand to beckon him downstairs and outside. With yesterday morning's little drama still fresh in his mind, Connor shook his head and walked back over to his bed.

"Co-nnooorrr," he heard again from behind him, Lydia singing his name like a line from a nursery rhyme to catch his attention. He turned on his heel and marched back over to the window. He looked out and beheld Lydia still there, still smiling, still beckoning him to come out of the house and join her.

"Come on out, sleepy head!" she shouted up to him jovially. "I want to show you something!"

Connor sighed deeply and melodramatically, and he knew at that moment that he was not going to get rid of her so he might as well just suck it up and go outside.

"Just a minute," he shouted down from his upstairs window, and proceeded to don his sneakers and a fresh T-shirt. Down the stairs he went and found himself outside where he saw that she beamed with happiness at his acceptance of her invitation.

"Hi Connor! How are you today?" she asked.

"Yeah, fine. What did you want to show me?" he replied, a little more petulantly than he intended, but Lydia did not pick up on his tone. Or she *did* but chose to ignore it.

"Come on, it's this way!" she said, starting off at a skip down the road and around the corner. He followed her and started to wonder if she was playing a trick on him and would at any moment just shout "tag, you're it!" and run away, but on she went. They proceeded down the next street and around another corner before Lydia led him into an alleyway between two sets of houses.

"Where are we going?" Connor asked in frustration, his arms stretched out horizontally at his sides.

"We're here; look!" she said, beaming once more, pointing to something unseen behind a large dumpster. Following the line of her outstretched finger and rounding the dumpster to behold whatever it was Lydia was so excited about - was it a doll, a bike, a pile of coloured chalks? - he jumped back aghast once he discovered the answer. There, curled up beside the dumpster, covered in dried blood, flies, and maggots, was a dead cat.

"Isn't he *beautiful*?" she asked, as if introducing her new-born child to its siblings for the first time. Connor didn't know what to say, let alone what to do.

"It's… Is that? It's dead, Lydia! It's crawling with maggots… Are you… Are you fucking sick or something?!" he shouted, cursing entirely out of character.

She noticed.

Her smile disappeared, her whole demeanour changing with the squaring of her shoulders and the stare in her dark eyes.

"Cursing is *bad*" she declared, emphasis pointedly in the final word. "Momma doesn't like it when children curse…."

"Enough, Lydia!" Connor interrupted, making to turn his back on Lydia, the dead cat, this whole bizarre scene, "I'm going home."

"Home?" she asked; a grin pulling at the corners of her mouth.

"*Home?*"

She started to laugh hysterically.

She laughed, and Connor ran.

Home.

Connor slammed the front door closed behind him as if fearing that the warm summer wind itself would steal him away at any second, and once again headed upstairs to the safety of his room. He kicked free his sneakers and sat on his bed as a shudder announced itself down his spine.

What was that all about?

Why did she laugh like that?

Who even is *she, anyway?*

Did she *kill that cat?*

All these thoughts and a thousand more flashed through his mind at once, and he closed his eyes, sucked in a deep breath, and blew them all out at once, unanswered though they may be.

Unanswered now, he thought, but that might have to change.

He whiled away the next few hours in his room, not even stopping to warm up his lunch. His nerves were shredded and he was convinced that *"Co-nnoorrr"* would ring out again at any second, Lydia having followed him home to demand his attention anew. But it didn't; nothing was sung from outside of his window, and nobody came calling.

His mother arrived home around 5pm - as per usual - and began to prepare their evening meal with a familiarity of routine which was now starting to grate on Connor, though it was probably just his mood talking. Lizzy opened the refrigerator to take out the vegetables and noticed that Connor's lunch was still in its blue Tupperware, untouched and uneaten by her son.

"Hey, Connor?"

"Yeah, Mom?"

"Have you eaten today? Your lunch is still here…" she said with concern.

"Oh… Yeah… I wasn't hungry." Connor said, thinking back to the afternoon spent in his room, on edge and in anticipation of a "Co-nnooorrr" from the window.

"Are you feeling okay? You're not sick are you?" she said, putting a palm to his forehead to check for a fever.

"I'm fine, Mom" he replied, but she didn't seem convinced. She took a thermometer from the medical supply cupboard and made as if to place it into his mouth, but he swiped it out of her hand with the back of his own.

"I said I'm *fine,* Mom!"

Connor locked eyes with his mother and no words passed between them for ten seconds or more until Connor's temper began to wane and he looked down at the ground with the beginnings of tears in his eyes.

"I'm sorry, I… I'm just tired. I didn't sleep well is all," he said in a quiet, timid voice. Lizzy took a step forward and embraced him, kissing him softly on the head.

"It's okay, kiddo… I know it's hard for you being on your own all day. But, hey, do you want to do me a favour tomorrow? My suit is in the dry cleaner's in town, and I need you to pick it up for me."

"Okay Mom." Connor agreed immediately, happy at the chance to do something, *anything,* other than sit in his room all day, or go outside and play with…

"Tell you what," his mother continued, "We've had a good month at the magazine, so what say I treat you to a new video game, huh?" she smiled.

"That's okay Mom, you don't have to," he replied, but she reached for her purse anyway.

"No, I mean it - here you go," she continued, handing him forty dollars. "While you're in town tomorrow, stop by the games store and treat yourself."

"Thanks Mom." he said, tears now replaced by a smile - his first genuine smile all day. Dinner was served within the hour and Connor and his mother were soon busy devouring the meal with a hunger which suggested they hadn't eaten all week.

"Oh, hey, I forgot to tell you; Tommy's mom is dropping him off the day after tomorrow, so you guys can hang out and play while we're working." Lizzy beamed at her son.

"Oh, cool, thanks Mom" he replied, now actually quite looking forward to hanging out with a kid his own age; a kid other than…

"Have you seen Lydia today?" his mom asked. He swallowed the mouthful of food he was enjoying and decided to massage the truth a little.

"Oh, yeah, this morning. We just played soccer and then she went home. Nothing much to report."

His mother seemed satisfied with his answer, and they continued to enjoy their meal with Connor's little *moment* now forgiven and forgotten.

What feelings of peace he had enjoyed with his mother that evening well and truly abandoned him come nightfall. Never having been prone to night terrors or even particularly bad dreams in the past, Connor's sleep was nevertheless troubled on this night.

He saw disjointed images of horror and decay haunted his sleeping mind. He saw the cat in the alley, the flies buzzing noisily about its exposed, greying flesh. He watched in horror as maggots crawled out from the empty voids where its eyes should have been. He could not look away as the maggots twisted and distorted, growing larger as he stood in terror on the spot. He tried to cry out as a face began to resolve itself upon the maggots' sickly, yellow flesh, the face of a young girl. The girl-maggot began to laugh hysterically, and dream-Connor found that, this time, he could not run.

He awoke tired and lethargic, and not without a dull feeling of dread in his bones. Nightmares half-remembered hung just beyond the reach of his waking mind, though their effects lingered like echoes in a tunnel.

He ate breakfast on autopilot, barely registering his actions or the taste of his cereal. He soon proceeded to shower and dress and decided to have a slow, leisurely walk into town instead of riding in on his bike. He slung his Batman satchel over his shoulder, locked the front door and stepped outside into the morning sunshine. Though he half expected Lydia to be waiting for him outside the door, this morning she was not.

He decided to check once more that he had definitely remembered to pick up the ticket his mom had left him for the dry cleaners. He opened up his wallet and satisfied himself that it was indeed tucked away neatly alongside his pocket money.

'Name: L.Harris, Collection: Wednesday August 12th 2020' it read, though no particular timeslot was specified.

To the bottom of Easter Street he proceeded, turning at the corner of Park Road. From there it was more or less a straight line into the small town centre, a walk of about thirty minutes in total.

Good, plenty of time to think.

Though last night's dreams had not lingered in his memory, the events of the previous day certainly had. The cat, the look of joy on Lydia's face at its discovery, the hysterical laughter which had seemingly exploded out of nowhere at the mere mention of home. He needed answers.

Lost in his thoughts, he arrived in town much sooner than he had expected. It had been a little while since he had last ventured here with his mother, and he had never been allowed to go by himself before. Maybe this was his mother's way of showing that she trusted him, trusted his judgement, of showing him that she knew, despite last night's outburst, he was not a little kid any more.

He intended to pick up his mom's suit last of all before heading back as he wanted to spend a little time just wandering the stores, enjoying the summer sunshine and the company of strangers. His first stop was the local electronic hardware store which happened to be owned by the same Mr Gallagher who had nearly run over his soccer ball days earlier. He was a gruff old man but had never been unnecessarily tough on Connor.

Wandering the aisles, Connor stopped to look at the shiny new video game consoles as well as a few really old ones he barely even recognised; "Retro" was the word for these, he knew, all black plastic and wires. The same went for music players, too; in addition to the usual assortment of MP3 players and iPods, Mr Gallagher sold CD players both stationary and portable, and even something called a "Walkman" which played not CDs, but "cassettes", whatever they were.

He browsed for a few minutes then decided to leave the store and had to pass Mr Gallagher on the way out. He was still a little embarrassed by the soccer ball incident, so he merely wished Mr

Gallagher a "good morning, sir," and gave a nod on his way out of the store.

"You be careful playing by those roads, Connor," Mr Gallagher said in response, not in a reproachful way, but as a Grandparent or kindly neighbour might. Connor could have just kept walking but instinct and his desire to solve the puzzle that was Lydia kicked in without his conscious brain really having time to argue with the decision.

"Yeah, I'm sorry about that Mr Gallagher. It was just, I took my eye of the ball for a moment, literally. My friend, see, she... Hey, can I ask you a question?" Connor was floundering a bit now, his nerves threatening to curtail this new line of enquiry.

"Sure but make it quick in case I get a *real* customer." Mr Gallagher smiled.

"My friend, I only just met her really, and was wondering... You've lived around here longer than my mom and me. Do you know anything about Lydia or her family?"

"Well, first of all, I think you mean *my mom and I,* Connor. A sunny day is no excuse for poor grammar. But as for a Lydia.... no. No. I can't say I know a Lydia. But then again it seems like there are more and more of you kids every day, so it's not surprising, really. There was one little girl a few years back, but... No never mind that. It can't be related."

"Okay, thanks again, sir." Connor said, nodding once more and leaving the cool store to once again brave the morning heat. His next stop was *Ready-Game-FIRE!*, which was just across the street from

Mr Gallagher's and his pace quickened excitedly as he crossed the street to spend his allowance money. Upon entering the store, he smiled as he was met by a wall of colours, sounds, neon display signs, and every video game he could ever possibly want; too bad he could only afford one or two today. He spent way more time in there than he did in the electronics store, perusing every aisle, picking up every box, devouring the cover art, and gazing lovingly at every carefully selected screenshot on the backs of those hallowed cases.

After nearly half an hour he had selected, paid for, and lovingly stowed in his satchel two new games - not *brand* new, but new to *him*. He was now eager to get home and play until his mother came home from work, so he made his way to the dry cleaner's post-haste. He entered the premises a few minutes later and handed in the ticket, collected his mother's suit, and headed off home in a much better mood than he had been in in days. The events of the previous morning were now all-but banished from his thoughts.

It wasn't until he rounded the corner back onto Easter Street that a vague uneasiness made its way once again into the pit of his stomach, and the sudden realisation that Lydia could be waiting for him outside of his house threatened to spoil his mood entirely. But waiting for him she was not; he did not see her once either going to or coming back from town, and he entered his house at a much more leisurely pace than he had upon leaving the alley and the dumpster the previous day.

With Lizzy's suit hung up in her room as instructed and a tall glass of juice with ice poured and placed on his bedside table, Connor opened his bag and took out his new games. He smiled as he chose which to play first and put his feet up on his bed, determined to and enjoy the rest of the day in peace.

Connor followed through on his plan and spent the rest of the morning and that whole afternoon in his room playing video games until Lizzy came home.

It was not long before dinner time was upon them once more, and both mother and son were soon sat in their usual positions around the table.

"Thanks for picking my suit up today, honey; did you have a good day?" she asked. Connor nodded while he swallowed a mouthful of food before adding words to his gesture.

"Yeah, Mom, I actually had a lot of fun today." She smiled at him - she had a habit of doing that - "That's great, Connor; you *do* seem in a better mood today."

And he was, he really was. But it wasn't going to last.

Lizzy was a little less frantic the following morning. The fact that Josephine was going to be dropping Tommy off and then driving them both into work gave her one less thing to fret over. She had gotten up early, took a much-needed shower, and dressed for work before she made breakfast for Connor and herself. She even had time for a second cup of coffee before she heard a car pull up outside their house.

"They're here kiddo," she said to Connor, despite the fact that his head had turned at the sound of the engine just as hers did. She stood up to greet them at the door and motioned for her son to do the same. "Morning Joey; hi Tommy." she said as the visitors entered the house.

"Good morning Mrs Harris; hey Connor." Tommy replied a little nervously. Similar greetings having been made all round, the ladies headed off toward the car and left the boys in the house, and Connor's usual regimen of daily instructions applied to their guest today, too.

"So," said Connor, attempting to break the ice "do you play soccer?" He was *really* hoping Tommy would say yes.

"Yeah, soccer is good," the red-haired boy replied. Connor grabbed the ball and they headed out into the morning son where the boys did as boys have always done - and will continue to do until the sun goes nova - and bonded over a soccer ball as if they had been friends their whole lives. They didn't play long before they had to go back inside for a drink and a rest given the heat.

"I *totally* won." said Tommy, punching Connor in the arm softly in jest.

"No way. If anything, I'd call it a tie." replied Connor with a similar thump. It felt good to have an actual friend to play with, and a male friend at that. Especially one who wasn't into dead cats and prone to bouts of creepy, hysterical laughter.

Once they felt suitably refreshed and rested, the boys chatted away about nothing and everything from soccer and video games to their moms' work and, for some reason, their fathers.

"My Dad is a pain in the ass," said Tommy "Strict, you know?"

"Not really… I never knew my Dad. He left when I was just a baby," replied Connor, and Tommy's cheeks turned almost the same shade of red to his hair.

"Oh, sorry man, I didn't know. Do you know why he left?" Immediately regretting the question and certain that Connor was not going to answer, Tommy made to hold up his hands in a *hey, you don't have to answer that* sort of gesture but found that Connor was happy to talk about the subject.

"No, it's okay. To be honest, no, I have no idea why he left. Mom never told me. I've tried to ask a few times, but she always just kind of avoids the question." Connor looked away, suddenly pensive and lost in his thoughts. Tommy seized the opportunity to take a leaf out of Lizzy's book and completely change the subject, and made a suggestion: "Hey, wanna go play some video games?"

Within five minutes they were in Connor's room, controllers in hand, trying to cram in as many games as they could before breaking for lunch. Connor really was having a good time and decided to let Tommy know it.

"It's cool to hang out, man. You should see if your mom would let you come over again, or I could come to your house some time." Tommy agreed; either would be cool.

"The only other person I've really hung out with since moving here is…. ah, you know what? Never mind." Connor decided it best not to mention Lydia right now.

"Who? Go on, tell me…. Is it a *girl*?" Tommy smiled, teasing.

"Actually yeah; her name is Lydia. She lives down the street and around the corner, but she's a little……odd" Connor replied.

"Odd how?" asked Tommy.

"Just…. Just odd; she bursts into tears for no reason one minute, then starts laughing hysterically the next. Just odd."

"Women." said Tommy, wisely.

Nodding, Connor continued "She even showed me a dead cat, called it *beautiful*. It had maggots coming out of its eyes and everything."

"Ewwww… Dude, that's sick. And not in a good way. We should totally go call for her."

"No!" said Connor, a little too quickly. "Sorry, um, no, it's cool. Maybe next time, huh? We only have two controllers, so, you know…" Satisfied with his friend's explanation, Tommy did not ask again.

The boys finished lunch and then headed back upstairs to continue their gaming marathon. Summer was in full swing, the sun blazing and the heat baking the very paving stones outside the Harris house, so naturally the two boys decided to sit indoors and play video games with the curtains closed.

Lizzy and Josephine were back before the boys knew it. The red-haired boy said his goodbyes, bumped fists with Connor, and they were gone. Seeing that the boys had clearly hit it off, Lizzy was pleased.

Maybe this is the start of something good for Connor, she thought.

Once their evening meal had been prepared, mother and son were once again sat across from each other discussing their respective days. Lizzy had reconsidered her position and decided to run with the story about the serial killer in England, though some of the gorier details had been omitted. Connor told his mother about playing soccer with Tommy and regaled her with tales of their video gaming exploits which she barely understood but she smiled and nodded encouragingly despite her obvious confusion. Following a brief lull in the conversation, Lizzy determined that Connor was chewing more than just his food.

"Everything okay, kiddo?" his mother asked, immediately sensing the weight of something pressing down on her son.

"Why did Dad leave, Mom?" he asked, seemingly from nowhere. It took Lizzy a moment or two to process the question. "Connor, I… what?"

"Dad. Why did he leave?"

"Connor, honey. I don't see that it matters, it…. It was grown-up stuff, okay? Husband and wife stuff" she replied, hoping that would be enough.

It wasn't.

"Husband and wife stuff? Mom, come on; I'm not a little kid any more, I want to know the truth!" Connor pressed.

"Yes you are, Connor Harris. You *are* still a kid, so drop it okay? Drop it."

The rest of the meal and the rest of the night in the Harris house played out in near silence.

As did the following morning.

Connor did not get up to have breakfast with his mother, who offered him only a cursory utterance of parting as she left for work. He sprung out of bed as soon as he heard her pulling out of the drive, ate some toast before getting showered and dressed, and was in the process of deciding how to spend the day when a familiar *"Co-nnooorrr,"* from his window startled him out of his thoughts. He knew what he was going to see before he even looked and there she was, standing outside his house waving up at him from the grass below.

"Lydia…" he said to nobody in particular.

Despite his misgivings about her mental state and temperament, he went outside to meet her in any case.

"Hi Connor! How are you today?" she beamed as she waved at him, childlike as ever.

"Hey…" he replied. "Where have you been, I haven't seen you in a couple of days?" Lydia tilted her head ever so slightly before replying.

"Oh, just to see my Daddy. I always visit my Daddy for a couple of days at this time of year."

Okay, that makes sense, Connor thought. "Where does he live?" he asked.

"Oh, he has a… um…what do you call it? A room?" she struggled.

"An apartment?" Connor offered.

"Yeah! Apartment! That's it. It's small. He doesn't like it very much."

"Cool," Connor said, more to fill the silence than anything else.

"Where's *your* Daddy? I see your Mom coming and going, but never your Daddy." Lydia asked earnestly.

"Oh, I um, I don't really have one… He left when I was just a baby."

Why does this keep coming up? He thought.

"Oh… that's sad," said Lydia, looking genuinely crestfallen. Then she looked up at him and smiled her menacing smile.

"Did he leave because your mom is a filthy, cock-sucking *whore*?" Connor felt as if he'd been punched in the guts. "What did you say?" he asked, though he had heard her perfectly well. Lydia was unfazed.

"Your Daddy; did he leave you because your mom is a dirty whore? Or did he just *hate you*?" she practically hissed the final two words.

"Get out of here! Go! Go on, leave me alone!" Connor screamed at Lydia with tears in his eyes. As he turned to run back home away from her, he heard her giggling behind him. He ran home as fast as he could and slammed the door shut, putting his back to it. He slid down the wooden door into a sitting position and couldn't hold back the tears which fell as easily as the autumn leaves which would soon litter the ground of Easter Street.

It took a few minutes for Connor to compose himself once more, and he eventually stood up knowing Lydia would already be gone before he'd even looked out of the window to confirm it. The rest of the day passed in something of a blur for Connor as a thousand questions rattled through his head.

Why did she say that?

Has she heard it from somebody?

Was she just repeating something she'd heard in a movie? If her momma wouldn't even let her play with other kids, he seriously doubted she'd let her watch *those* kinds of movies.

Why did she say that? Round and round in his head this conundrum went, tormenting and confusing him in equal measure until his body stepped in with a timely assist. Legs like lead, eyelids heavy, and his very *soul* exhausted, Connor laid down and slept through what remained of the morning, all the way through to late afternoon.

He had not long woken when his mother returned home from work. To her credit, she was clearly trying to extend an olive branch by acting as if everything was okay and back to normal between them.

"Hey honey," she called to Connor who, seizing the opportunity and secretly needing his mother's affection much more than he'd ever let on at this point, replied in kind.

"Hi Mom; how was your day?"

Back to normal indeed, and both mother and son were grateful for this though neither gave voice to it; they didn't have to.

Later, with their evening meal served and tall glasses of wine and juice poured respectively, Harris senior and Harris junior set about their evening conversation.

"How was your day, kiddo?"

"Oh, not bad… I saw Lydia for a little bit this morning, but then I just came back and had a long nap; this heat, you know?" Connor replied, trying to steer the conversation away from Lydia.

"How is she? You haven't mentioned her in a couple of days."

"She's okay. She said she went to visit her Dad, so I didn't actually see her for a couple of days. She also said… actually never mind." Connor decided against acknowledging the girl's accusations.

"Said what?" his mother replied.

"Said, um… that her Dad lives by himself, that's all."

"Oh. Hey, honey…" his mother shuffled uncomfortably in her chair just a little. "I need to run something by you, is that okay?" Looking a little confused, Connor nodded.

"Sure, Mom. What is it?"

"You know Jeremy? From the magazine? Well he's offered to take me out for dinner and drinks tomorrow night and I um, I said yes." Connor took a second or two to process the information.

"Like, a date?" he asked.

"Yeah, honey… like a date. Is that okay?"

"Sure. Sure it is Mom; I hope you have fun." he replied.

Later that night, once the

dishes had been cleared away and mother and son had retired to their rooms for the night, Connor lay awake, thinking.

A date. A date with a man. A date with drinks and dancing. Like a whore. Like a cock-sucking whore…

He tried to forcibly shake these thoughts from his mind as he turned over and attempted to court sleep. His efforts were in vain, though, and Lydia's smiling face plagued his dreams.

Were there an Academy Award for *Best Dramatic Performance By A Son In A Kitchen*, Connor would have won hands down. Despite his restless, tormented sleep and Lydia's words impressing themselves upon his mind, not to mention the fact that for some reason he just wasn't okay with his Mom dating in any case, he didn't show it.

He wished his mother a good day at work and assured her - once again - that he knew the drill. A little while later, after he had showered and dressed and had sneaked in a video game or two for good measure, he decided to go and make a quick snack before heading outside. He didn't want to see Lydia but he still felt like going out today, even if it was just for a walk.

He wasn't in the mood for chocolate or anything sweet at this time of morning so instead decided to just make himself a sandwich. He took the ham from the fridge and the freshly baked loaf of bread from the cupboard, gauged the thickness of the slices he wanted and began carving the bread.

He hissed a sharp breath through his teeth as he accidentally guided the serrated bread knife through his finger. The cut wasn't too bad, but there was a lot of blood. He knew he could have just dealt with it himself but he also knew that his mother would kill him if he didn't follow the rules. So, wrapping his finger in a wad of tissue, he made his way across the road to Mr and Mr Kingsley's.

Mr Kingsley, an elderly African American man with grey hair and an even greyer beard, answered Connor's knocking almost immediately and invited him in with a smile noticing the bloodied digit.

"Bread knife, huh? Yeah, we've all done it, son. Nanna!" he shouted, referring to his wife by the name her grandchildren used. "Could you please come and help Connor and I?" Into the kitchen she came, her hair almost the same colour as her husband's and wearing a kindly smile - a Nanna, indeed.

A few minutes later and Connor was all patched up. The old couple had given him a tall glass of cola and the three were sat in the living room making small talk, chatting about the weather, Connor's school, and whether or not he had seen his friends this summer.

"Well, my friend Tommy came over yesterday. We played soccer and video games. It was cool. I've also met Lydia this summer, from around the corner." A look of mild alarm came over Mr Kingsley's face.

"Did you say Lydia?"

Connor nodded and answered politely as he had been raised to do.

"Yes sir, Lydia. I don't actually know her surname, but she's a little bit younger than me with blonde hair. We've played together in the street a few times. Do you know her?"

Mrs Kingsley nudged her husband almost imperceptibly, but he got the message alright.

"No. Can't say I know anybody named Lydia," he replied, a bead of sweat making its presence known upon his forehead. "But hey!" he said more brightly "tell me about those video games...."

A few minutes later with his finger all wrapped up and his cola finished, Connor thanked the couple for their hospitality and excused himself. He left their house and waved goodbye before turning and heading home. His back was to them now, so he did not see the dark, concerned look which passed between the Kingsleys.

Once he was home again, Connor discarded the bloodied bread and finished making the sandwich he'd started, this time with more success. He was sat at the table tucking into his snack when he heard "Co-nnooorrr," from outside. He closed his eyes for a few seconds and sighed heavily to himself, then got up and walked to the window.

Lydia was standing outside with a smile on her face which suggested nothing bad had ever transpired between them; no harsh words spoken, no unpleasant experiences shared. He found that strangely disarming about her so went outside in spite of himself.

"Hi Connor, how are you today?" she asked, happily.

He held up his bandaged finger. "Okay, apart from this."

She laughed at him, a genuine, childish laugh as opposed to her previous maniacal cackle.

"What did you do, silly?" she asked, chuckling.

"I cut myself slicing bread. It was bad." he responded, almost proud of his *war wound.*

"Come on, let's go play." she said, turning on her heel and heading off down the street. He followed, though he had no idea what today's *play* consisted of. He did know, instinctively, that it was bound to be something weird and boy, was he right about that.

Lydia led him down Easter Street once more, around the corner and toward the alley when Connor's alarm bells started to ring. She carried on straight past the alley, however, and instead stopped outside of number 17, Park Road.

"This is my house." she declared, brightly.

The garden was overgrown and the windows were dirty and smeared on the outside as if only a cursory effort had been made to maintain the appearance of a nice, family home. It was nothing like Connor's, with its manicured lawns and spotless windows. A thought suddenly dawned on Connor.

"Is your momma home? If she sees you playing with me…"

Lydia chuckled. "No, silly. She's not home. She's at Church."

Church? On a Friday? Connor thought…. *That's a bit weird. But then everything about Lydia is weird.*

"Come, see…" Lydia said, and made her way through the open gate, down the side of the house, and into the back garden. It too was overgrown and generally unkempt. She led him to the centre of the grass, and the old familiar sense of dread dawned upon Connor as he beheld a crow.

Not a live, vibrant, impressive creature, but one lying on its side, clearly in pain, with one wing twitching as if this would only allow it to fly away from here, away from *her*.

"Jesus!" Connor said, wide-eyed, looking away from the stricken bird and back to Lydia who held his gaze, unblinking.

"He's hurt. You have to kill him," she said flatly.

Connor recoiled in horror at the mere suggestion.

"What? I have to what?!"

"Kill him. He's hurt." she replied, matter-of-fact once more. She pointed toward their crumbling garden wall where a few bricks had come loose.

"Use those." she said.

"No, I…. I can't!" Connor protested.

"You have to. He's hurt. You *have* to."

"What about your mom, when she comes home?" he said, thinking to pass the responsibility on to somebody - anybody - else.

"She could be gone for hours, Connor. *You* have to kill him. He's hurt. Use the brick." Lydia continued to hold his gaze.

"I…I…" Connor took a tentative step toward the old wall, and Lydia shifted gears.

"DO IT!!!" she screamed "DO IT! HE'S HURT, CONNOR, KILL HIM! USE THE BRICK! KILL HIM! *KILL HIM!*"

Overwhelmed and seemingly caught, trance-like by Lydia's encouragement, Connor grabbed a brick and, in one fluid motion, brought it down heavily on the crow's head.

How he ended up back in his room he couldn't quite remember; the last thing he *could* remember was the bird's wing falling to the ground, still at last. He unwrapped his bandaged finger, and sat for what seemed like forever, silently staring at the cut and the blood which poured openly from it once more.

He sat there a while unable to really *think,* still numbed by his actions and the terrible way he'd been encouraged by a screaming Lydia.

What have I done? was the one clear thought he kept coming back to. He replayed the event over and over in his mind, on the one hand rationalising that he had done the right thing and put the poor creature out of its misery, but on the other hand he knew all too well that he could have called somebody, called a professional to come and help. Maybe even just Mr Kingsley.

Lydia, he thought. *It's always Lydia.*

That she was strange, he knew without doubt. That her schooling arrangement was as bizarre as the rules on friendships which her mother enforced, he was also certain. But there was something else, *something* just didn't add up.

Connor's musings were interrupted by the sound of his mother coming home.

Early, he noted. *Date night.*

Lizzy all but took the stairs two at a time, such was the hurry she was in to get ready for her date with Jeremy. She checked in on her son and immediately noticed his finger, so he forestalled her inevitable questioning by hastily explaining the morning bread knife incident and his subsequent cola with the Kingsleys. She seemed satisfied with his explanation so informed him that she had brought home take-out for him; a huge, meat-topped pizza. The mere mention of the word "pizza" set his stomach off growling like an angry bear, and it dawned on him that he had skipped lunch again.

Within forty-five minutes, his mother was all ready for her date sporting full make-up, black dress, and high heeled red shoes. He had never seen her like this before and suddenly understood why Jeremy would want to take her for a meal; she was pretty for forty.

She kissed him goodbye and left in the waiting taxi. He was alone now; Connor had the run of the house - again - but this time at night. His head suddenly filled with all manner of exciting things he could do over these next few hours, but he instead did what any self-respecting eleven year old boy would do: he reverted to type, ate his pizza and went to his room to play video games.

He had fun for a little while but, try as he might - and he did try - he just couldn't shake Lydia from his thoughts.

Whore…cock sucker…Kill it…Use the brick…KILL IT…Whore… Filthy cock-sucker…

He slammed the game controller down on his bed, took a deep breath and decided to just try and get some sleep. He must have needed it too, because it wasn't until his mother returned at around

10:45pm that he awoke a little groggy. He made his way downstairs to greet her and found her sat at the kitchen table with a glass of red wine in her hand.

Not her first tonight, he noted.

The only light in the room was coming from the hood of the cooker; she had clearly tried not to wake him.

"Hey, honey! What are you still doing up?" She wasn't exactly slurring her words, but was definitely a little merry. Noting the glassiness to her eyes, the smudged lipstick, and creased dress, he could tell that her date had gone well.

"I just came to see if you had a good night, that's all," he said, not entirely truthfully.

"Yeah, it was fun. We ate, we had some wine, did a little dancing, then Jeremy put me in a cab home. He's nice; you'll like him." she smiled, taking a long, satisfied sip of her wine.

"Mom, why did Dad leave?" he asked.

His mother, clearly not expecting this question, put her glass on the table and stared long and hard at her son. Her inquisitive son.

Her *petulant* son.

"How many more times? We've been over this, Connor."

"No, we haven't. Every time I ask you avoid the question or change the subject. Why won't you just tell me?" he pressed, his voice now raised.

"Connor…" she began.

"Did he leave because you're a whore? A dirty, cock-sucking whore?"

Before she even knew what was happening, Lizzy had stood up, closed the distance to Connor in one long stride, and slapped him - slapped him *hard* - across the cheek. The two stared at each other for what seemed like an eternity.

"How dare you…?" she whispered.

"How *dare you*? whispering no longer.

"Your father was a piece of *shit*… a lying, cheating, gambling, drunk, lazy piece of shit!"

"Mom…"

"No, Connor. You wanted to know. Well, here I fucking go…" He had finally broken her, it seemed.

"Your father was a useless, lazy fuck who drank and gambled away what little money we had managed to save, and spent more time in motel rooms with young, skinny sluts than he *ever* did at home… and *I'm* the whore? And when he found out I was pregnant… Oh boy…"

"All I've ever done is protect you, Connor, that's all I've ever tried to do and *I'm* the bad guy?"

"I'm sorry Mom." Connor said with tears now streaming openly down his face. "It's just that, it's just… Lydia said…"

"Lydia?! *Lydia* said?" his mother yelled furiously.

"I've had just about enough of this Lydia nonsense… A girl you've only known for five minutes and I've never so much as even met. Come here…"

She grabbed him by the collar and marched him out of the house.

"Where does she live? *Where*, Connor?"

Connor was virtually paralysed with fear - he'd never seen this side of his mother before - he pointed forwards, put one foot in front of the other and slowly led the way.

Down Easter Street they proceeded, around the corner and onto Park Road, past the dark alley, and on to number seventeen. Connor indicated the house with the name *Jameson* stencilled on the mailbox out front and Lizzy strode confidently up to the door and knocked for all she was worth despite it now being past 11pm.

A light flickered to life inside and the muffled sound of rattling keys and a tell-tale *click* preceded the door opening. Standing in her dressing gown, dark eyed and clearly confused by the sight she beheld, was a woman not far from Lizzy's age who, judging by her blonde hair, was Lydia's *momma*.

"What is this? Who are you? Do you know what time it is?" said Mrs Jameson to Lizzy and Connor.

"Your Daughter, where is she?" demanded Lizzy.

"What...?" replied Mrs Jameson.

"Your daughter, Lydia, she's been leading my son astray for weeks now, and has been throwing some foul, hurtful accusations around; I want to speak to her, *now*."

Mrs Jameson stood, face unmoving, staring at her late-night callers before she finally responded in a quiet, almost timid voice.

"What is this? Who are you? Where do you get off? *This* week of all weeks?" All previous timidity now abandoned, she continued.

"Is this some kind of sick fucking joke? Get out of here! Go on, get out of here before I call the 'cops!" she shouted.

"Not until I've spoken to Lydia." said Connor's mom, standing her ground.

"My Lydia has been dead for three years, you fucking bitch! What sort of sick joke is this?"

Connor and his mother stood there on the Jamesons' doorstep, dumbfounded, unable to make sense of what they were hearing from the grief-stricken woman in front of them, when something caught Connor's eye. Just a flicker of movement behind Mrs Jameson, half-hidden in the shadows of the dark hallway beyond.

The flicker resolved itself into a shape, and there, pale skinned, her jaw hanging low in a nightmarish approximation of a silent scream, staring at him with unseeing, black eyes, stood Lydia.

Excerpt from the Topeka Capital-Journal, August 12th, 2017

Police and local volunteers are involved in a huge search operation following the mysterious disappearance of ten-year-old local girl, Lydia Jameson.

Lydia was last seen by her parents in the family home when they put her to bed on the night of August 10th but was not in her room the following morning.

Local law enforcement agencies are now conducting a thorough door-to-door canvass to ascertain if anybody in the area noticed anything or anybody unusual in the last 24 to 48 hours…

Excerpt from the Topeka Capital-Journal, August 13th, 2017

Tragedy struck a small rural community today as the body of ten-year-old Lydia Jameson was discovered hidden in her own family's barn on private land just outside of town.

Police had previously been treating her disappearance as a home invasion and kidnapping, but the location of the grim discovery has now thrown that theory into doubt and new avenues of investigation are being pursued...

Excerpt from the Topeka Capital-Journal, August 16th, 2017

In a shocking development in the Lydia Jameson case, police have today arrested Nathan Jameson, forty-three, for the rape and murder of the ten-year-old whose body was found at the family barn a few days ago.

Friends and relatives of the deceased have told our reporters that the girl was deeply troubled and was often prone to violent outbursts. Lydia was home-schooled by her mother (Ally, forty-one) and was not permitted to mix with other children due to her increasingly worrying behaviour. If what we are now hearing about her father is true, however, then perhaps the girl's behaviour was merely the manifestation of the trauma she had endured throughout her short life...

Excerpt from the Topeka Capital-Journal, September 10th, 2017

It took the jury only thirty-five minutes to return a Guilty verdict today in the trial of Nathan Jameson, accused of the rape and murder of his own daughter, Lydia.

The judge handed down a life sentence to Jameson who is to be transferred to El Dorado Correctional Facility later today to begin his long sentence. A spokesman for the Jameson family told our reporters…

El Dorado Correctional Facility, August 12th, 2021

Nathan Jameson sat silently in the dark as he always did this time of year. Alone in his small cell, his room, his *apartment,* he wept quietly to himself and stared into the dark corner, not wanting to see what he knew was coming.

He checked his watch and ignored the piss which ran openly down his orange jump-suited leg.

"Hi Daddy," he heard from the shadows.

UNEXPECTED ITEM

This isn't so bad, thought Gary as he sat in the small but well-lit office of the enormous PriceCo supermarket. *It definitely beats sitting in portacabins on freezing cold fucking building sites all night.*

It was already nearly midnight on a dull, cold Saturday, but Gary felt surprisingly alert despite his comfortable chair and the small heater at his feet which would have tempted lesser beings into the welcoming arms of sleep. But Gary was a *pro*, he'd been working as a security guard for years now, and his time-served in the job was almost as impressive as the gut he had gained in the process.

Here he now found himself, working nights in an enormous supermarket which had been plunged into darkness but for the light in Gary's office. He still found it strange that a supermarket should need to employ an overnight security guard, but ever since the little girl had gone missing on that sunny Summer afternoon, the locals had taken to protesting and vandalising the store.

It was the CCTV footage that somehow found its way into the hands of the press that really *did it*; the little girl with red hair, wearing a floral yellow dress could be seen as clear as the day outside in tears, asking the green-shirted shop assistants for help finding her parents. But help they did not, and instead dismissed the girl as somebody else's problem. After all, the baked beans weren't going to stack themselves…

No trace of little Tanya Smethwick had been seen since. So here Gary sat with a book in hand, occasionally glancing away from the epic fantasy tale titled *Legends of Aclevion* in which he was engrossed, and looking instead to the live feed on his monitors to confirm his suspicions that nothing was happening and he was essentially being paid to do fuck all.

1am; time to make my rounds, he thought, folding over the corner of his page and putting the book down.

He picked up his torch and his plastic pass and stood up. His job now was to visit each little sensor located at intervals around the store and touch his pass to electronically log the evidence to his superiors that he was actually doing his job and not just sleeping in his comfortable chair. He hardly even heard the *beep* anymore.

He passed by the front desk.

Beep.

He turned around the corner toward the magazines and birthday cards.

Beep.

Onwards he went, leaving the wrapping paper behind him and heading towards deodorants and moisturisers.

Beep.

Turning on his heel, he set off toward the cooked meats.

Crash!

The noise was loud, and Gary thought it had come from the back of the supermarket, the opposite end to where he now stood still and straight, on full alert.

"Fuck, what was that?" he said out loud to nobody.

He remained in place, with only the rhythmic pounding of his pulse in his ears for company. Or so he thought.

He shook his head to clear the cobwebs and told himself to *get a fucking grip* and do his job. He tentatively put one foot in front of the other and began making his way toward the far end of the store.

The end which housed the loading bay doors.

On he went, passing the cooked meats and ready meals. Further still past the tinned goods and confectionary…

Another sound; not a crash this time so much as a scuffle followed by a *sloshing* noise.

Gary was in back in full control of his faculties and pressed on, determined.

His suspicions had had started to grow as to the source of the sounds, and as he rounded the corner of the tea and coffee aisle and onto the wines and spirits, he confirmed them.

"For god's sake, man! How many times do we have to do this same fucking dance?"

Old *Willie the Wino* ceased his crazed guzzling of the screw-top shiraz he had broken into the store to acquire long enough to squint into Gary's torch light.

"Ah, go and fuck a bin bag, you fat fuckin'... Fat... Go get fucked!" he slurred and stammered at Gary.

"Nice, really classy Willie. I mean, if you're gonna steal wine, at least steal the expensive stuff, you cheap old maniac. Right, on your feet."

"Fuck your feet, you fat fuck…"

"Willie, *on-your-feet*. Up. Now."

Willie grudgingly obliged and offered Gary his best approximation of standing up, which was at very least effective if not remotely graceful.

Gary took Willie by the arm and led him back outside through the door he had clearly broken in via.

"Can I at least have my bottle?" he asked.

"What? No! Of course not! Now go on, go home, and don't let me catch you here again."

"The only thing you're gonna catch is diabetes, you fat fuck."

"Nice, Willie. Really nice." Said Gary as he made the doors secure once more.

He stood with his hands on his hips, slowly shaking his head and sighed deeply in the renewed silence of the darkened PriceCo supermarket.

I might as well continue my rounds, he thought at last and turned around to pick up where he left off.

Beep…

Beep…

Beep…

Beep…

Giggle. Tap tap tap tap…

Gary's blood froze in his veins and his heart lurched into his throat as he registered the tiny, high-pitched giggle and the footsteps coming from directly behind him. He stood, unmoving, not even daring to blink let alone turn around, and all was silence. Whatever had been *tap tap tapping* toward him had now stopped.

Gary swallowed hard and tried to force his breathing to slow down, his pulse to steady and his nerves to calm. Mentally counting down, he decided the best thing to do was to simply turn and look.

He was probably imagining it anyway.

3, 2, 1... He turned.

He only saw it for a split-second, but it was enough for every hair on his body to stand rigid.

Every instinct within him told him to *run*.

Every nerve and sense was on full red alert.

He saw a little girl running away down an aisle.

A little girl with red hair, wearing a floral yellow dress.

To his credit, it only took him moments to once again force himself into action, regaining control of his sense by sheer force of will. He set off to follow.

"Tanya?" he shouted into the darkness, and as he gave chase the tapping of plimsoles on tile and the high-pitched giggling renewed.

On he pressed down another aisle and around another corner, nearly knocking over a stack of cat food.

"Tanya? Tanya wait! It's okay, my name is Gary, I won't hurt you!"

He was breathing hard by this point and, not for the first time, lamenting the weight he carried.

Giggle…

That one sounded different; it sounded like it was coming from…

The escalators!

The blur of colour Gary was chasing had seemingly made its way to the escalators and was now moving to the upstairs level which was home to menswear and the small café.

"Tanya, stop! Please! It's okay! I'm here to help! I'm going to call your mum and dad to come get you! They'll be so pleased to see you! Tanya?"

The giggling stopped abruptly, and Gary could no longer hear the sound of the girl running.

It was probably just his imagination, but he could have sworn they stopped at the mention of her parents.

Silence. Silence and darkness were back, but they no longer offered any comfort to Gary.

"Tanya?" he spoke to the darkness, slowly and softly making his way forward once more.

"Tanya? Are you still there, honey? If you're hiding, it's okay; nobody is going to hu-"

She rushed out of here hiding spot and straight at Gary, who only had a second to turn his torch toward her before she had gone barrelling into him at full speed.

But the brief moment was enough. Enough time for Gary to register, to his horror, the burning red eyes, the deathly grey skin, and the deep, angry slash where a pretty young girl's round, pink face once resided; the innocent smile of a child now replaced with an angry, demonic grimace.

The otherworldliness of her countenance was matched only by her strength and ferocity, and she sent Gary tumbling over the safety railing to the ground floor below. The creature which had once been 9-year-old Tanya Smethwick walked calmly toward the safety railing and peered over the top to behold her handiwork.

Gary, PriceCo security guard, lay dead at a grotesque angle, his neck snapped and cruelly displaced as his bulk had landed atop him by Tanya's hand.

She stared into his dull eyes and savoured the last embers of terror which still lingered there, at least for the moment.

"I have brought you another, Master." She said.

"Good," came a voice from the darkness; a deep voice, an *ancient* voice which sounded like nothing living, mor akin it was to rock scraped upon stone.

"I have to admit you were right, my child," it continued.

Demon Tanya inclined here head in deference to her lord.

"Should one seek to gorge oneself upon pathetic, broken, human souls; should one wish to feast on the despair and pain of the living; should one desire to wash down the anguish with a hearty draught of fear, one need look no further than a supermarket on a Saturday."

THE DOLLMAKER

"They still haven't found her, huh?" Geoffrey said to Lana as he entered the living room to find her watching the evening news on TV. She hadn't heard him climb the creaky old basement stairs, didn't register the click of the lock on his studio door, and was unaware of his approach, engrossed as she was in the news.

"No. It's been months; poor girl." she responded.

The newsreader affected a sombre tone as he provided viewers with an update on the disappearance of twenty-four-year-old Alexa Maxwell who had not been seen since the turn of the year.

"...are issuing a further appeal to the public for information, and are urging any witnesses or anybody who may know anything - however small - about the missing girl to please come forward and contact the police immediately. Once again, Alexa Maxwell has shoulder length brown hair, a distinctive scar above her left eye from a roller-skating accident, a tattoo of a raven on her left forearm, and police are asking people to be on the lookout for these distinguishing characteristics..."

Geoffrey sat down on the sofa next to Lana and leaned over to kiss her gently on the head, pulling part of her winter blanket over his own cold legs to stave off the late November chill,

"The poor parents. It must be hard." he said.

"Yes, it's just awful. Especially with Christmas coming up and all." replied Lana, wiping away a tear.

"Are you all finished?" she asked, smelling the soap on his hands.

"Yes, all done for the night, babe." He replied, squeezing her. "Clean as a whistle down there. I'm gonna go take a shower and climb straight into bed, okay? Don't be up too late."

"I won't." she replied absently, never taking her eyes off the TV.

"It's just awful."

Lana awoke the following morning feeling refreshed but a little troubled. Geoffrey had already left for work, leaving her in bed. The house was quiet and the only sounds she could hear were coming from outside as cars went by and children shouted and played in the street.

Outside, she thought with a slight shudder. She had meant to venture beyond these four walls today, even if it were just for a walk or to visit the local shop to purchase something she knew she didn't need or even want; she just needed to *go outside*. Lana was not agoraphobic as such - at least she didn't think she was - she just had a natural aversion to the outdoors and the company of strangers. For his part, as long as she and Geoffrey had been together, he had always encouraged her to take the plunge and venture outside, even just for a walk around the block, and she had been sure that today would be the day. Lana did not work; she didn't have to thanks to Geoffrey's salary, and she rationalised that her social anxiety prevented her from insisting on bringing home a second income should she be so inclined. Besides, Geoffrey was old fashioned for forty-two and he secretly quite liked her being at home.

She exhaled the early morning weariness from her bones and slid out of bed, not unlike a child being forced to rise by a persistent parent, before picking up her thick-framed spectacles from her bedside table, donning her dressing gown, and making her way downstairs and into the kitchen.

Coffee, the thought dominated her mind and she knew she would be in no position to make an informed decision before she'd had a cup or three. She turned and faced the room as the kettle boiled, taking in her surroundings though she knew the room by heart. She had not lived here that long in the grand scheme of things having only recently moved in with Geoffrey, but she was comfortable here, she *belonged* here. The click from the kettle snapped her out of her revelry and she stirred the contents of her cup. The steam rose prominently in the early morning chill, and she suddenly felt an overwhelming sense of dread at the prospect of going out into the world today. She heaved herself down onto the sofa and drank her coffee slowly with the TV remaining off; she had neither the attention span nor the patience this morning.

You don't have to go far, she told herself, *just to the end of the street and back.*

But what if somebody tries to talk to me? What then? said another part of her.

What then? You talk back, that's what; Jesus, it's not difficult.

No... No, that's too much, I can't do that. At least not today. Maybe tomorrow.

That's what you said when we had this same conversation yesterday.

Lana shook her head, forcibly calling time on her internal debate and continued to drink her coffee in both external and internal silence. Once her cup was empty, she checked her watch and realised it was still early - 7:20am - but she was not only up and awake but restless now too, thanks to the argument she had just had with herself. Deciding there was no way she would be able to sleep were she to crawl back into bed, she settled on grabbing an early shower.

A few minutes later, Lana stood with her eyes squeezed shut as the hot water cascaded onto her face and head, flowing freely over her body and warming her to the bone. Even here, cradled in the embrace of the hot water which fended off the outside cold and caused every nearby window to steam up with condensation, she knew she really *should* try to go out. At length, she decided she'd had enough and turned off the shower, which was the cue for the cold air from the open bathroom window to make its inexorable charge and immediately chill Lana, undoing the good work the shower had put in to warm her up. Once she was dried and had replaced her dressing gown, she brushed her teeth and proceeded with her daily ritual of putting in her contact lenses - a chore for which Geoffrey did not have the stomach.

It's funny how some men get a kick out of violent movies and video games, cheering every gunshot and stab wound, but can't watch their own partner put her contacts in without squirming, she reflected, and not for the first time.

Lenses in, she proceeded to her dressing room and threw on a pair of jogging bottoms and a t-shirt before drying her hair. Her hair was shortly cropped, so it took very little time to towel the blonde locks dry. She applied a little wax and completed her signature messy, pixie-cut look; she was still fairly confident that she was not in fact going to leave the house today, so a quick tousle would suffice. One thing she would not slack on, however, was her makeup; she always made a point of applying her makeup, housebound or not.

Makeup and contact lenses, she thought to herself.

I have some *standards, at least.*

Fifteen minutes later, Lana was once again downstairs on the sofa with a coffee in hand.

I need to cut down on the caffeine, she thought, knowing all too well that she would not in fact cut down. She switched the TV on and punched in the number for the 24hr news, as she always did around this time of the morning. As she had expected, the station was soon playing a repeat of the previous night's police appeal to help trace the missing girl, framing it as her parents' Christmas wish to have their little girl "back home safe, where she belongs."

The story tugged at Lana in a way she didn't expect; there was something about the girl which resonated with her, an abstract feeling she couldn't quite give form nor name to. Something on the tip of her tongue; just beyond her peripheral vision.

I mean, we're about the same age and same height, she mused.

And I haven't seen my own parents in months either, so…

Confident that she had hit the nail on the head, she shook the thought free from her mind and tried instead to formulate a plan for the rest of the day.

I actually could do with quickly popping to the shop for a few things, she realised, thinking ahead to preparing their evening meal.

Hmm… Is that really such a good idea? You know how they stared last time, another part of her argued.

But it won't be like last time. I just need a couple of things, that's all; there and back before you know it.

Okay, well on your head be it. You know you shouldn't. Especially not alone.

Lana decided she would finish her coffee before making any decisions and drained the last of her cup while the news reader showed another photo of the missing girl, Alexa. Deciding enough was enough, she turned off the TV and marched into the kitchen, practically slamming her cup down into the sink. She set her brow and pursed her lips as if this would tangibly aid her in the process and proceeded upstairs.

Don't do… she banished the voice.

Think about… another one she cut off before it could build any real internal momentum.

What if someone… she bit down on her lip to silence the latest of her demon thoughts.

Just wait a second, it's all over… this one she forcibly shook from her mind and closed her eyes in a bid to keep her fears in check, at least until she changed out of her jogging bottoms and into a pair of jeans, a jacket, and a woolly hat.

As soon as she had finished changing into her more weather-appropriate clothes, she slid on her winter boots, grabbed a large shoulder bag, and headed back downstairs more determined than ever to leave the house and go to the shop at the end of the street.

Fuck you, fuck you all, she told the other Lanas, the ones she had spent the last fifteen minutes fighting against, the ones she was constantly struggling to lock away inside the small, dark boxes she stored inside her head.

Sometimes she was even successful.

I can do this; I will *do this.*

Closing and locking the front door behind her, Lana turned to face her street and was momentarily taken aback by the appearance of her own breath as she exhaled long and heavily into the cold morning air.

Well, you're outside, I guess we'll soon find out… they said.

Break it down, one bit at a time, she told herself as she struggled to comprehend the dawning enormity of an early morning trip to the shop. She had already devised a plan ahead of time, and decided to treat the journey as more of a relay race, hitting certain mental checkpoints before handing over the baton for the next small leg of the trip. So, on she went. She strode confidently down the path and turned left onto the street, not breaking stride as she made her way toward the junction at which she waited, looked both ways, then crossed the road.

Stage 1 complete.

She felt a little better at the thought of her home, her sanctuary, now being what seemed like miles – *leagues* – behind her, though in reality was barely two-hundred meters. As Lana pressed on, she became aware of a mother coming toward her with a pushchair in front. She tensed, and felt as if an arrow had been fired directly into her gut, but again she did not falter. As she approached the lady, she offered her approximation of a neighbourly smile.

"Morning." Said Lana, to which the lady replied in kind before continuing on her way.

That wasn't so bad, thought Lana as she struggled to contain the bile which had risen in her throat at this encounter. Acting on instinct rather than conscious thought, she cast a leisurely glance over her shoulder.

And immediately wished she hadn't.

The lady with the pushchair had stopped and was similarly looking over her own shoulder in Lana's direction. It was not the fact of her stopping which bothered Lana, but the look of confusion on the lady's face and the brazenness with which she wore it. Their eyes met for a split second and the other lady averted her gaze, embarrassed, and continued on her way.

Lana knew she was pretty, knew that her haircut and style choices marked her out as a little bit different from the beige and grey masses, but she just couldn't abide the stares. Her pace quickened as she made the next leg of her journey, then the next, head down and avoiding wandering eyes. She passed parents taking their children to school, and smartly dressed men and women heading off to work in expensive cars. More than once she became aware of eyes lingering on her for a moment or two longer than would ordinarily be considered polite, but still she headed onwards.

At length she found herself outside of the convenience store and was relieved when the automatic doors opened and then closed behind her.

See? What did we tell you?

Shut up; I can do this.

No, Lana, you can't. They know what you are.

I said shut up!

Haha… As if it were that simple, Lana. How long before one of them actually puts it together?

Shut.Up.

They see it in your face. They know what you've done…

"I said shut the fuck up!" she shouted out aloud.

The store's overweight and very hungover-looking security guard trundled over to her, red in the face from the shock of her outburst.

"Miss? Is everything okay?" he asked with a raised eyebrow.

This is too much; I can't do this.

"I… leave me alone." She managed through the beginnings of tears, and turned on her heel and ran out of the shop in the direction of her and Geoffrey's home. Again, she passed random people simply going about their lives, who were visibly startled by the appearance of a girl running down the street in tears at this time of the morning.

But that's not all, is it Lana?

She ignored the mocking voices until she was back inside her home; she immediately slid down the closed door into a sitting position, and she wept.

Stop it! Leave me alone!

Alone? You are alone. You've never been so alone, Lana. Even when he is here, you are alone.

Why are you doing this to me?

Doing this to you? What about what you did to her; what you both did to her?

No, that's not true! Geoffrey didn't… He, we… We didn't do anything!

Really? Then why does he spend so much time down there?

That's just where he works! It's his… his studio!

Studio… Oh, Lana… You truly do belong here.

Stop it! Shut up!

She regained her feet and ran down the hallway, not stopping to cast so much as a spare, fleeting glance at the locked door which led to the basement. She took the stairs two at a time and jumped straight into bed, still fully clothed and wearing her winter boots.

"Lana? Lana, honey? Are you here?"

At the sound of Geoffrey's voice and the familiar sound of him kicking off his work boots and putting his keys in the little bowl they kept on the side table, she sprung out of bed and all-but ran down the stairs to meet him.

In one glance he took in the redness in her face, the puffiness around her eyes, and the fact that she was still fully dressed, boots and all. She threw her arms around him and sobbed deeply into his shoulder.

"Hey, hey, hey! Slow down; what happened?"

"They know, they all know! They were looking at me, all of them… They know! And then the other Lanas, they… they said…"

"Hey, okay, stop. Come here."

He gently pried her arms from the vice-like grip they held around his neck and led her to the living room. Once she was on the sofa next to him, he took her by the hand.

"We've talked about this, babe. Nobody is staring. They might be looking at you, but they're not staring. As for "knowing", there's nothing to know, honey."

"I know, but… The others, they…"

"The others aren't real, okay? Other Lanas? No. There's only one Lana; there's only you. I know you sometimes get confused, but…"

"No, Geoffrey." she bit back, shoving his hands away. "I'm not confused, I know what they all think of me. Are they right?"

Geoffrey took a deep breath, then blew it out slowly to bring some measure of composure to his rapidly darkening mood.

"What time did you go out?" he asked.

"Early… school run…"

"Have you been in bed the whole day? In your clothes and boots?"

"Yes, Geoffrey, I have. What the fuck do you expect?"

"Okay. Here's what we're gonna do, okay Lana? I'm going to go and run you a nice, hot bath, and pour you a glass of that red you like."

"Geoffrey, I…"

"Don't interrupt me. I'll pour you a glass, let you relax in the tub for a while, and I'll be downstairs, okay? There are a few things I've been meaning to do down there."

"In the basement?"

"Yeah, of course; the studio. Why do you ask?" replied Goeffrey, his brow wrinkled in confusion.

"Nothing… I'm just confused, I guess. What are you working on?" Lana asked, forcing a smile.

"Hm? Oh, just the eyes on the latest doll. I just can't seem to get the damn things right, you know? But I brought home some new enamel paints from the workshop, so maybe. Oh, I forgot to tell you!" he beamed.

"I've actually been experimenting with some new pigments, too, and this one colour I shipped in from Lithuania of all places, it… Ah, sorry honey. It's boring, I know."

This time her smile was genuine. She loved him; she really, truly loved him, and it warmed her heart to hear him talk about his work with such passion.

He loved his work, and had put quite literal blood, sweat, and tears into making his business a success. But for all his success he was not popular with the locals, and there was a small part of Lana's subconscious which suspected, though she would never consciously give it voice, that the stares and the glances she received had as much to do with *him* as they did with her.

Some people just found it odd that a grown man would choose to make a living creating 1:1 scale, made-to-order dolls.

The water was scolding hot, and the wine had been chilled to perfection. Most discerning human beings would consider it sacrilegious to fridge-chill a Merlot, but that was how Lana preferred it, and it had never tasted better to her than right now amongst the steam and bubbles.

The only sound she could hear was the subtle popping of bubbles as she moved her body beneath the surface of the water, not so much for cleansing nor comfort, but merely to feel its heat roll and roil across her skin. Though she could not hear it at this distance, she imagined that she could hear Geoffrey hard at work in the basement two floors below her, the sound of his breathing as he worked with tools in hand, the smell of the paint and the chemicals he used in his work, the chill of the air which crept in even below ground-level.

She felt her heart lurch at the thought, and felt a heat which was not born of water and wine swirl within the pit of her stomach. She stood up, threw back the rest of the wine in her glass in one gulp, and threw her towel around herself without stopping to dry.

Geoffrey held his breath in concentration with an inexplicably fine paintbrush in his steady, unshaking hand. To casual observers, he would have appeared as the protagonist in some macabre comedy sketch, in his magnifying goggles and paint-stained apron, applying the most delicate of brush strokes to the iris of a life sized doll, laid out as stiff as a board on his work table.

He was so deep in concentration that the sound of the basement door opening nearly gave him a heart attack, and he whipped off his goggles to behold a wet Lana dressed in nothing but a towel making her way intently toward him.

"Lana?" he asked, but she did not reply in words.

Before she had cleared the last stair and stepped fully into the basement, she had dropped her towel. She covered the distance between them in two strides and reached straight for his belt. Before Geoffrey could even register what was happening, she was on her knees in front of him, taking him into her mouth with bathwater and bubbles still in her hair and running down her back and shoulders.

She stood up, and helped him remove his clothes in record time, then shoved the work-in-progress doll off of the worktable and onto the floor. She climbed up onto the now vacant table and parted her legs, her eyes boring into his. Geoffrey did not need a second invitation as he likewise jumped up onto the table and into his waiting girl.

The doll had hit the ground with a dull thud, which neither Lana nor Geoffrey paid any heed to. In a basement whose walls were lined with full scale, unclothed, female human dolls like some strange honour guard, one lying on the ground was of little concern.

The doll had landed on its front with its unmoving, expressionless face to the ground, so neither Lana nor Geoffrey saw the tear it shed; a tear stained in an immaculate new pigment which had recently been imported from Lithuania.

The following morning saw Lana wake up happy and refreshed. She had all-but forgotten the trauma of the previous day and was looking forward to spending the day with Geoffrey. She turned her head on her pillow to face him, and he woke slowly at the touch of her fingers in his hair.

"Morning, sleepyhead."

"Hey… what time is it?" Geoffrey replied groggily.

"9:30. I thought I'd let you sleep a little. It *is* Saturday after all.

"Yeah." He replied, propping himself up on his elbows and shaking his head to banish the cobwebs.

"I thought we could order in some lunch and just curl up in front of the TV today. Whaddya say?"

"Ah, I'm sorry babe, no-can-do; I've got a delivery coming in today and I really need to finish the doll."

Lanas head dropped almost imperceptibly at Geoffrey's words, but she quickly regained her composure.

"That's okay; want some help?" she offered.

Geoffrey beamed back at her, somewhat taken aback by her offer.

"Really? I thought you… You know its *completion day,* right? Finishing touches, and all that?"

"Yeah, that's okay. I want to help; I think I should be more involved anyway. We're a team, you and I."

Geoffrey leaned over and kissed her forehead.

"We *are* a team. I'm so glad you realise that. Hey, I'll tell you what; how about you help me today, and I'll take you out tonight for drinks?"

Lanas face darkened at the suggestion of going outside, especially out for drinks around other people.

People who would look.

People who would stare and point and whisper…

"Gefforey, I… you know I…"

"Don't worry, it'll be okay. I know the perfect place. It'll be dark, we can sit in our own little booth away from everybody else. In fact, it'll be more than fine, it'll be great. I love you; you do know that?"

"Of course. I love you too; I'm your Lana, remember?" she blew out a long breath before throwing Geoffrey a grin and a nod of assent.

"Right, okay then," she said definitively. "I'm gonna hit the shower, you can make the coffee."

Lana sprung out of bed and headed straight for the bathroom, excitement, topped with just a tinge of apprehension, coursing through her veins.

I'm finally gonna help him
I finally get to finish one!
Then we'll go out and drink and maybe even dance…
I really do *belong here.*

The knocking at the door sent a jolt of excitement through both Lana and Geoffrey, and the dollmaker jumped up from the couch in his eagerness, almost spilling his coffee in the process. Lana followed him out of the living room and headed toward the kitchen to make a fresh pot whilst Geoffrey thanked the delivery man for the unassuming and innocuous-looking package. Geoffrey headed straight downstairs with parcel in hand, and Lana followed him with their fresh coffee.

She found him eagerly unwrapping the packaging and opening the box, discarding layer upon layer of bubble-wrap and protective paper stuffing, and noted the glee in his eyes as he withdrew the small vials of clear liquid from within.

"Finally," he said, grinning. "It took longer than usual to arrive this time. But, hey-ho, I suppose it comes with the territory. Not like you can just get this stuff over the counter, huh?"

"Which one is that?" Lana asked.

"What, this?" he replied, holding the vial up to the basement light. "*Tetrodotoxin.* They get it from pufferfish, of all things."

"Is that the one that… you know?"

"No; this one just paralyses them so I can paint their eyes and plasticise them. That sometimes finishes them anyway, so I don't always need the other one. Speaking of which, let's get her up here."

Geoffrey walked casually to the human analogue which still lay face down on the basement floor where it had landed the previous night. He turned it over onto its back, took the shoulders, and motioned for Lana to take the feet. On the count of three, they lifted the doll up onto the table.

"Fuck, it's wearing off. This arrived right on time." Geoffrey said, picking up the tetrodotoxin vial and reaching for a syringe. He carefully inspected the doll in front of him on the worktable, and his brow furrowed as he noticed it's lips quivering and made out the barely audible whimpering noise it was making.

"This one's almost ready to ship." he said to Lana as he inserted the needle into the doll's arm and emptied the contents into its bloodstream. He let the toxin do its work for a few minutes while he and Lana sipped at their coffee. At length, he placed his cup on the nearest worktop and poked and prodded at the doll. He satisfied himself that the doll was indeed paralysed once more and set to work.

Before too long, he had finished painting the eyes the exact shade of green his client had specified, and was just finishing up applying the layers of hot, flesh-coloured plastic to its skin.

Had the tetrodotoxin not arrived this morning, this part would have been *loud*.

"Okay, here; quickly, before it sets hard." said Geoffrey, handing Lana a new syringe and an altogether different vial of clear liquid.

"How much?" she asked, piercing the lid with the needle.

"2ml should do it. Make it 3 if you want to be sure. And it's best to go for the neck."

Lana nodded her understanding and withdrew the liquid from the vial. Her eyes flashed up at the doll's and was proud of herself for not balking at the sight of the tears openly running down its cheeks. She strode confidently to the head of the table and pieced the rapidly hardening skin of the doll's neck with the needle, emptying its contents into the carotid artery.

Neither Lana nor Geoffrey spoke as they stood and waited for the botulinum toxin to do its work. Lana cast her eyes around the studio, noting the wooden boxes which lined the walls, each one ready to ship. Each one bound for a customer. Each one containing a doll.

Geoffrey took a stethoscope from a drawer and placed the diaphragm upon the doll's chest.

"Congratulations, you completed one." he smiled up at Lana. "Now, I just need to get this one boxed up and clean down the equipment. We'll grab a bite to eat, and we'll be elbow-deep in cocktails before you know it! Oh, that reminds me!" Geoffrey withdrew a fresh vial of tetrodotoxin from the box and took a fresh syringe from the drawer.

"Can I put these in your bag when we go out tonight? The next client wants a redhead."

A few hours had passed since Lana helped Geoffrey to complete the doll. She was proud of herself and proud of Geoffrey. He was good at what he did, and his customers paid him handsomely for his services. His dolls were special, unique, and he had perfected his craft over the years. He must have sold seventy or eighty dolls at this point, and each new city he moved to presented new opportunities for both customers and *materials*.

Lana had picked out her outfit for the evening and had already secreted Geoffrey's vial and syringe inside a hard-shell glasses case inside her handbag. She liked to keep the TV on in the background while she got herself ready, though she wasn't really paying much attention to it. A mindless and unoriginal gameshow had just ended, and the evening news was now her soundtrack as she tied her towel tight around herself and contemplated her makeup options.

"...still have not given up hope of finding her, but with no fresh leads and no witnesses coming forward, Alexa Maxwell's family and friends must be preparing for the worst. Once again, if anybody has any information about the disappearance of the twenty-four-year old..."

Lana reached for the remote and turned off the TV, cutting the newsreader dead in his tracks.

You can't ignore it, you know. Said one of the other Lana's inside her head.

"Shut up, leave me alone."

They know... They all know.

"I said shut up!"

What makes you so special? Why aren't you in one of those boxes?

"He loves me! I'm his Lana!"

So was I, once…We all were. Until he painted our eyes.

"No, that's not true. Stop this. I'm his Lana."

Are you? Are you really?

"I said stop it!!!"

"Hey, you okay babe?" said Geoffrey, poking his head around the bedroom door.

"Yeah, I'm fine, just talking to myself is all." She replied with a smile which did not quite reach her eyes.

"Okay, well I'm gonna jump in the shower and then we'll be ready to go."

"Cool, cool."

Lana turned to face the mirror, pausing momentarily in anticipation of a renewed assault from the voices in her mind, but they had thankfully fallen silent. She stared at herself in the mirror for a few minutes as she calmed her breathing and likewise calmed her mind.

Satisfied that the voices were now long gone, she set about drying her hair; a task which was so much quicker and easier since she cut off her shoulder length, brunette locks.

Next, she took her makeup brush and applied a liberal helping of concealer. This she used to cover up the raven tattoo on her left forearm, before topping up the brush and applying the makeup to the scar above her left eye.

The scar she had received from a roller-skating accident a few years back.

She strode over to the wardrobe and brushed her fingers against the silk of her dress, a dress which once belonged to Geoffrey's late wife, Lana. She removed her towel and began to dress, loving the way the silk felt against her skin, and turned once more to the mirror.

There we go, perfect. She thought as she appraised her look.

Geoffrey loves me, and I love him.

He takes care of me.

I belong here.

I'm his Lana.

For now, said what remained of Alexa Maxwell.

Printed in Great Britain
by Amazon